critical acclaim for

Screaming Hawk

Patton Boyle crafts a completely surprising narrative about a true conversion experience and its inescapable paradoxes. As a Christian at mid-life foundering in dry religion, his hero learns to fly and scream like a hawk under the tutelage of a wry Native American teacher, who shares his hard-won secrets, shows us how to reset the boundaries of self, belief, and Spirit, and shape new life.

Richard Leviton
Senior Writer for *Yoga Journal*
and author of *The Imagination of Pentecost*

Screaming Hawk is spirtually beautiful and exciting — it all seems too fantastic for words, yet too real to deny. All who aspire to spiritual growth will identify with his trials and their transforming simplicity.

The Rev. Donald L. Keefauver
United Methodist Church, Retired

Screaming Hawk is one of the most, direct, simple, and pure articulations of spiritual truth I have read. It is strong medicine, carrying raw transformational power for all spiritually hungry minds with open hearts and the desire to travel more deeply into mystical wisdom.

Bradford Keeney
Professor, Graduate Programs in Professional Psychology, St. Thomas University,
author of *The Aesthetics of Change* and *Shaking Out the Spirits:
A Psychotherapist's Entry into the Healing Mysteries of Global Shamanism*

Screaming Hawk is a wonderful book filled with insights into the spiritual life, native American spirituality, teaching and learning. It is enjoyable reading and holds the reader's attention from beginning to end.

The Rev. John H. Westerhoff III
author of *Will Our Children Have Faith?*,
Director of the Institute for Pastoral Studies, St. Luke's Episcopal Church, Atlanta,
and retired Professor of Theology and Christian Nurture, Duke Divinity School

Screaming Hawk

FLYING EAGLE'S TRAINING OF A MYSTIC WARRIOR

Patton Boyle

Station Hill Press

Published by Station Hill Literary Editions, under the Institute for Publishing Arts, Inc., Barrytown, New York 12507. Station Hill Literary Editions is supported in part by grants from the National Endowment for the Arts, a Federal Agency in Washington, D.C., and by the New York State Council on the Arts.

Distributed by The Talman Company, 131 Spring Street, Suite 201E-N, New York, New York 10012.

Front cover painting by Stephen Hickman.
Cover and book design by Susan Quasha, with assistance from Vicki Hickman.

Library of Congress Cataloging-in Publication Data

Boyle, Patton L.
   Screaming Hawk : the training of a mystic warrior : a visionary narrative / by Patton L. Boyle.
     p.   cm.
   ISBN 0-88268-159-1 : $9.95
   1. Spiritual life—Fiction. 2. Indians of North America—Religion and mythology—Fiction I. Title.
PS3552.0929S37   1994
813'.54—dc20   93-48778
                                                    CIP

Manufactured in the United States of America.

Author's Preface

In many respects this book is not my own creation. At no point in the process of writing it did I have any outline and most of the time I had no awareness of what the next sentence or, at times, even the next word would be. But the words came day after day along with a compelling urge to write them down. There was a sense of adventure as the story and teachings unfolded before me each morning. Even now it seems as though I am reading someone else's work. I marvel at Flying Eagle's teachings. They contain a wisdom that is not my own.

The Great Spirit speaks to me through this book, as Flying Eagle would say, "not through the words themselves but in the silence between the words." May you too hear the voice of the Spirit in the silence between the words.

◢ 1 ◣

"But I don't want to be a warrior," I protested. "I believe in peace."

Flying Eagle made no reply at first. The fire, which was mostly coals by now, flared briefly, revealing some of the many wrinkles in his aged face. "Many warriors do not know that they are warriors," he said. "When you came to our village and asked me to teach you about the Spirit I was skeptical. Many have come before you asking to learn our ways. I did not waste my time on them. They were curious but they were not really committed to learning the ways of the Spirit. But there is something different about you. I have been observing you with my people. They like you. They tell me that your heart is good. I have been meditating about your request. Last night, Star Man came to me. I told him that I was considering accepting you as my student. He was pleased. He told me that you are the one he had spoken of many years ago and that I must teach you the way of the warrior.

If you want to learn the ways of the Spirit you must follow your true path and learn to be a warrior. You think you already know what a warrior is, but you don't. Because you do not yet know who you are, you will question many times whether this is the proper path for your journey. There is no other way. Weigh your decision carefully. If you still want to be my student, I am willing to teach you. But if not, you must leave."

I felt excited, confused and scared. I longed to be Flying Eagle's student but the idea of becoming a warrior went against everything I believed in. I had come because I wanted to learn but now I was afraid, afraid of what I might learn about the Spirit and about myself. We sat in silence again. The fire popped, releasing a single golden spark to rise upward toward the waiting stars.

"Who is Star Man?" I asked, finally.

Flying Eagle smiled. "We will begin your instruction. I will tell you about the first time I met Star Man." He took a deep breath as though he were rolling back the years and continued, "It was many years ago, long before the great fire that destroyed our village. I was young at the time, not quite sure of myself and still uncertain of my manhood. I was sitting alone by a fire late at night when he approached silently from out of the darkness and stood facing me. His presence startled me. At first I thought he must be a visitor from the other village, but when I looked closely at him, even in the flickering of the firelight, I could tell that he was no ordinary man.

"His hair was pure white and it sparkled here and there as do the stars on a clear winter night. He wore one eagle feather in his head band. The feather was perfectly formed and yet appeared to be made of raw silver.

"He spoke to me. He told me many things about my people and many things about the Great Spirit. He talked with me all through that night.

"As dawn was starting to show its first light in the east he told me that I would be a great medicine man among my people and that at some point a white man whose heart was good would come to me and ask to learn our ways and that I must teach him what I know about medicine and life with the Great Spirit. Then Star Man vanished and I was alone.

"Through the years many have come to me and asked to learn about the Spirit. But none of them had a good heart. They wanted to take from us but they did not know how to give. I told them nothing. Now I am old and you too have come and asked me to tell you about the Spirit. Star Man told me you would come. I will teach you what you want to know, but it will take much time. There are many things that a warrior must learn. You must learn how to listen in a new way but you must also learn how to wait. Now it is time to wait."

Without saying good night, he stood up and headed back to the village, leaving me alone with my thoughts and my fears.

2

Flying Eagle did not speak to me again for four days. I continued to occupy my time by assisting the men of the village with a variety of odd jobs and maintenance work on the wood frame buildings. I worked and I waited. Finally Flying Eagle came to me where I was stacking wood and said, "That can wait. We will talk now."

He led me in silence about a quarter of a mile into the forest and we sat down, Indian style, on the crisp leaves under a large tree. After about five minutes of silence he spoke.

"I have been wondering how to help you understand the things that I will be telling you without confusing you about the nature of truth. I have been thinking about this since we last talked by the fire. What I am going to explain to you now you will forget many times. I will have to remind you often of that which the Indian seems to know by nature. The White Man thinks that truth is found in facts, in words and sentences that can be memorized or written down. That is not so. You can memorize all that I tell you and still not learn the truth. You can question me and try to figure out how this piece of information fits with that piece. You can come up with theories that explain things to your rational mind. But your theories and explanations will not help you to find the truth in my words to you.

"Last night I remembered a visit we had many years ago from a Christian missionary. He was an angry and troubled man who had no interest in learning our ways or learning what we know of the Great Spirit. He came to our village to prove us wrong and to collect Indian converts to his ideas in order to prove his own importance. I talked with him for two hours one afternoon. He told me many things that I had to believe to be 'saved', but he seemed to know little of the ways of the Spirit from his own experience. He left angry because I did not accept all of his ideas and I was not interested in joining his church. But he said one thing that I think may be helpful to you now. We were talking about the Bible or 'Word of God', as he called it. I asked how it could be the word of God when it was not written in the language of my people and said things in strange and confusing ways. He said that the printed words themselves are not the word of God but that God speaks to us between the words. He said that as you study the words in the book God speaks to your heart in your own language. When he said that, I told him that he would make a good Indian. I meant it as a compliment. I could tell that he was insulted. He left angry and went to another village where I am told that he converted one 73 year old widow who had not been right in the head for many years. Our people smile when they tell stories about that missionary, but I remember what he said about God's word coming forth from between the words in the Bible. What he said about that is wisdom. What I will tell you is like that. My words are not the truth. Learning them will not give you the truth. I will tell you things about the animals speaking to people that are not true to a man of science but are more deeply true than a man of science can understand. You must learn to hear the truth coming through the silence between my words. If you learn to do that you will enter the world of the Spirit. If you try to take my words as truth you will never find the truth. Indians know this. When you learn it you will know things that can not be spoken and understand things that can not be explained."

He stood up abruptly, turned and headed back to the village. I sensed that he expected me to remain where I was. I sat there in silence a long time, thinking about what he had said and feeling a strange mixture of excitement, because my apprenticeship had begun, and dread of the unknown.

❧ 3 ❧

In our next session he opened with a prayer to the Great Spirit. He spoke in his own language. I could not understand what he said. Then he turned to me and said, "Did you understand what I told you the last time we met?"

I nodded my head.

"Good," he said. He took another deep breath like the one he had taken that night by the fire and began: "Much of what Star Man told me about life with the Great Spirit I did not understand at the time. But I remembered his words and with time came to experience for myself much of what he told me. He said that the animals are our friends and that they have much to teach us about the way of the Spirit. Each kind of animal has its own type of experience of the ways of the Spirit. The hawk has a way of being that is different from the eagle's or the bear's. I could teach you about each animal and its way of being but it is better for you to learn how to talk to the animals yourself and learn from them rather than through another man. Each man has many different ways that he can be with the Spirit but each kind of animal has only one way, its own way, to be with the Spirit. Man gets confused because there are so many ways to be with the Spirit and some of them seem to be the opposite of other ways. Each animal knows its own way and can teach you that one particular way so you will not be confused. Learn from the eagle how to be an eagle. Many men try to be an eagle and a rabbit at the same time. It doesn't work. A man can have many ways to relate to the Spirit but he should use only one at a time. The animals can teach you how to follow one way at a time, how to be an eagle and then later how to be a rabbit or a fox or a deer. All of the animals know something of the Great Spirit. Learn from them, but follow only one way at a time."

"How do I talk to an animal?" I asked.

"You must go to where the animal is, to where the animal lives in the forest or in the fields. Go there and the animal will come to you. You must wait for the animal to come to you. You must not go to the animal. Hunters go to the animals. Men of wisdom wait for the animals to come to them. When the animal comes you must wait until it is ready and then you can talk. You will know when the animal is ready. Sometimes it takes much waiting. When the animal is ready you can talk to it. Tell it what you want to know, what you want it to teach you. Then you must wait again. The animal will speak to you when the animal is ready and when you are ready. Sometimes it takes much waiting. Sometimes it doesn't. When the animal speaks you must listen between its words. The animal will not teach you through its words but between its words. It is as I told you before. You can not learn of the spirit through words, only between the words. The Spirit does not come in words and the truth is not revealed in words. The truth must be experienced.

Many people try to borrow the truth from another person by listening to words and understanding them. But the truth is never in the words or in the understanding. The truth must be experienced. The words can point you in the direction of the truth and your understanding can help you to use the truth once you have got it, but the truth is not in the words or in the understanding. You can not borrow the truth from others through their words. The truth comes in the silence between the words. It is grasped and experienced with the heart.

White Men know little of the animal world because they are unwilling to wait and they do not know how to listen. They think that they can learn the truth from the words in books or from studying science. But they can not learn about the Spirit in those ways. They must learn to listen. The animals will only teach those who have learned how to listen between the words."

"I have heard that Indians have power animals who speak to them. Can you tell me about that now?"

"Every person has a power animal. But not everyone knows his power animal. Few White People talk to their power animals or even know that they have one. In order to talk to your power animal you must learn how to listen. Your power animal can teach you how to get in touch with your own inner power. Your power animal can teach you how to be yourself, how to use your inner power and how to speak to your own spirit."

The next day I went into the forest to talk to an animal. I found what I thought to be a comfortable spot and sat down to wait. I waited a long time. I saw some birds and squirrels in the distance but none of them came to me. After several hours I returned to the village. When I saw Flying Eagle I told him about my experience, or lack of it. He said, "You are not yet ready to talk to the animals. You went with curiosity in your mind. You went to see if what I was telling you about the animals was true and to find out what they would say to you. You did not go with a question in your heart and you are not yet ready to listen between the words for the truth.

"Many years ago my people were facing big problems. I was confused and I went to speak to the mountain lion about it. I sat all day and all night waiting. In the morning the animal came to me. I was afraid at first. It was a powerful animal and I had no weapons. Sometimes an Indian has doubts too. The animal came and stood close to me and told me not to be afraid. Then we talked. It told me that the problems we faced would pass but that I had to go to the leaders of my people and tell them that they were wrong and that the problems in the tribe would not improve until they changed their minds. I don't know whether I was more afraid of the mountain lion or of the chief, but I went to him and told him what the mountain lion had told me. He received it as wisdom and called a council. At the council we resolved the differences we had in the tribe. Things were better for my people after that."

"Is the mountain lion your power animal?" I asked.

"No. I did not go to find out how to be more truly myself. I went to solve a problem that was being faced by our tribe. The mountain lion is known to have wisdom for my people. My power animal is not the mountain lion."

I was just about to ask him another question about power animals when he walked away. I felt frustrated. I don't like to wait for answers to my questions. Flying Eagle could tell that I wanted to know much more about power animals and yet he was deliberately making we wait. Why?

Then it occurred to me that he was forcing me to experience my impatience with him. Could it be that my impatience was one of the issues that was keeping me from being able to talk to the animals? I realized that it was. I felt embarrassed and returned to my chores with a deepened respect for Flying Eagle as a teacher.

❧ 4 ☙

The next time Flying Eagle talked to me he returned to the subject he had avoided in our conversation two days before. "You asked about power animals. It is not just your impatience that is a problem; it is your curiosity that is a problem as well. You want to learn about power animals and you want to learn about my power animal. You want to learn the truth through my words instead of experiencing it yourself. You can not find the truth through what I tell you. Truth can only be grasped through experience. In order to listen between the words you must be ready to experience what you find there. Go back to the forest and wait."

I did what he said. I went back to the forest and waited. I did not mind waiting at first. It was pleasant. The sun filtered though the trees creating patches of sunlight on the forest floor. I sat in relative comfort with the sun on my back and enjoyed the peace of the forest. I thought about what Flying Eagle had been saying and I waited expectantly.

The sun went down. It started to get chilly, so I scooped away the leaves with my foot and built a small fire with some dry twigs and branches. I sat down again and continued to wait.

The fire made the chill manageable. It was pleasant to watch the glowing embers and flickering flames. I continued to wait. Later in the evening it clouded over. I could no longer see the stars when I looked for them through breaks in the canopy of leaves and branches over my head. The earlier feeling of adventure was gradually replaced by a sense of total isolation. A few hours before sun rise it started to rain. The fire didn't help much. I was cold and wet and miserable. Nothing happened. No animals came to me. Around ten A.M. I finally gave up and returned to the village in defeat.

Flying eagle sent me into the forest every afternoon for the next week and a half to wait. Nothing happened except that I grew more content with my task and even started to look forward to my afternoons alone in the forest. Each evening before sun down Flying Eagle would find me in the forest regardless of where I chose to wait and would say "Enough for today." We would walk back to the village together in silence.

Once I asked him how he was able to find me in the forest. He laughed and said, "When you walk through the forest you leave a trail as wide as a moose in heat."

The eleventh afternoon Flying Eagle did not come. As the darkness was closing in I scooped out a fire place and prepared for the night. It occurred to me that Flying Eagle might have forgotten about me or been unable to find me this time. I thought about it, but quickly decided that whatever he was up to was undoubtedly deliberate on his part. I sat and waited.

This time I felt a strange calm; I was content to wait for another week if necessary. I thought about the animals in the forest and how different their lives were from mine, no clocks, no money, no taxes. I thought about how often I had seen birds sitting on a branch, waiting. I thought about the other animals of the forest and how often they seemed to be waiting. I felt a strange kinship with the animals. They spend so much of their lives waiting and now I too was waiting. I was content to wait, to wait with them in their world for whatever was to unfold. My curiosity and questions seemed to move into the background; it was enough just to be, to be myself, and to wait in the forest.

The night seemed to pass quickly. An hour or so after sunrise I heard a different sound from the quick, staccato noises made by the birds and squirrels as they moved about. The slower, more plodding sound got closer and then, he was there. An eight point buck walked slowly but confidently up to where I was and stopped about ten feet away. He looked directly at me. I was an intruder in his world but he showed no signs of fear. We looked at each other for perhaps five minutes. And then it happened. The deer spoke to me. It was one of the strangest experiences of my life. The deer spoke to me. There were no words, no sounds, but it was absolutely unmistakable. It was as clear as if he had spoken directly into my ear.

"You have come with questions," he said.

"Yes," I said, speaking out loud, but feeling at the same time that it was totally unnecessary to use my voice.

"I will answer some of them."

"I want to know about the world of the animals and how it relates to my world as a human."

"That is not easy to answer," he said. "You have not yet had enough experience in our world for me to tell you in ways that you will understand. Our world is not like your world and you can not understand it with your mind; you must experience it with your heart. You must become a part of our world or you will never understand what I tell you."

I had a strange feeling that I was beginning to experience what he was talking about already. It felt as if I were talking to him deer to deer. That in meeting him and talking to him I had entered his world and had become a deer. It was as though I knew from experience what it was like to live in the forest and run across the fields and drink water from the mountain streams and to experience the presence of the Great Spirit as a deer.

"I have a strange feeling that in some way I am a deer at this moment."

"You are." he said. "That is what happens when humans talk to us as you are doing now. You become one with us. You have become a deer."

"Are you my power animal?" I asked.

"No. I am not here to teach you about your own inner power. I am here to teach you about the world of the animals. If you want to meet your power animal you must do that at another time. Your power animal will come when you want to encounter yourself."

"Tell me about your relationship with the Great Spirit." I said.

"The Great Spirit is gentle and kind. It tells us when it is time to prepare for the change of seasons and how to raise our young and it tells us which men to fear in the forest. It told me not to fear you, that you were here on a quest for truth and that I should speak to you. The Spirit provides us with food and brings the rain that gives us water. The Spirit provides for us so we can live in the forest in peace without killing other animals for food. The Spirit gives us life and it is the Spirit who brings us back to health when we are sick. And it is the Spirit who receives us when we die. The Spirit gives us everything that we need."

"How do you experience the Spirit differently from other kinds of animals? What is special about experiencing the Spirit as a deer?"

"Deer live in peace with other animals. The spirit teaches us how to live in peace but it is not so with all animals. Some animals are taught to hunt by the Spirit. They learn how to defend their territory and how to fight. Some men think that fighting is against the will of the Spirit but fighting is only against the will of the Spirit for a man of peace. Not all people are men of peace; some are warriors and need to rely on the Spirit to teach them how to fight just as the Spirit teaches us how not to fight. A deer must be true to its own nature. It is our nature to be peaceful. It is the nature of some animals to be warriors. Men are the same. You want to be a man of peace, but you could choose to be a warrior and, at times in your life, you will need to be a warrior in order to fulfill the will of the Spirit for your life. Animals are consistent in the way they experience the Spirit. In the world of men, choices must be made, and at times some men of peace are called by the Spirit to become warriors. There is much confusion about this in your world. The bear can teach you about this because the bear is an animal of peace in most situations, but the bear becomes a warrior when it needs meat to live and when its young are in danger. Men must choose their own path. Animals have their path provided them by the Spirit. It is when a man does not choose his path that problems arise. Some men do not choose to be warriors or men of peace; they let their emotions control them. They get angry and act like warriors without choosing the path of a warrior. When that happens they do not fulfill the role of the warrior, they only act the part. They destroy things but they do not fulfill the warrior's mission. Do you understand?"

"Partly," I said, "but I'm not sure I understood what you just said about emotions and about fulfilling the role."

"Emotions should not determine a man's direction. Feelings are important and need to be experienced, but they should not be what determines a man's course of action. A man should not become a warrior because he feels anger. He should choose the path of the warrior because it is right for him. When a man becomes a warrior because he is angry, then his role becomes the expression of anger rather than the true spiritual role of the warrior. If a man tries to take on the role of a man of peace because he is afraid of violence, his role becomes the avoidance of his fear instead of the true role of a man of peace, to bring peace. We deer are not peaceful because we are afraid. We are peaceful because that is our nature; that is the role that the Great Spirit has provided us. We are peaceful when we are being ourselves. We can feel fear, but we feel it when our peacefulness is threatened. We feel fear when it is time to run, when we are not among animals of peace or men of peace. I have no fear now because at this time you are peaceful and I can trust you to do me no violence. I can be myself, an animal of peace, in your presence. A true man of peace is not peaceful because he feels peaceful. He is peaceful because he has chosen that path. Men have a choice. We do not."

ﺳ 5 ﺲ

That evening around 6:00 P.M. I was awakened by Flying Eagle gently shaking my shoulder. I had returned from the forest that morning and gone directly to bed.

"I brought you some supper," he said. "Tell me about the deer."

"How did you know about the deer?" I asked in amazement.

"When I was young I had the same kind of questions you have now. I met a deer in the forest and we talked. Yesterday you seemed to be ready to meet the deer. He did come to you, didn't he?"

"Yes."

"Tell me what he said."

I told Flying Eagle all that the deer had said to me.

"Did you become a deer?" he asked.

"Yes in a strange sort of way. At one point I started to feel as if I were a deer. It wasn't a physical change, but it was as though I could think like a deer and remember experiences that I had not had as a man. It was a strange but wonderful feeling. It lasted for perhaps five minutes and then started to fade away."

"Sometimes men actually change and become animals physically, but we will talk more of that at another time. You have done well. Get some rest. We will talk more later."

He left my room. I went back to sleep and awakened at dawn feeling rested and fit. I got dressed and returned to the spot where I had been in the forest the previous day. To my surprise the deer was waiting for me. I sat down and waited.

"We did not finish our conversation yesterday," he said. "There was danger and I had to leave. I was going to tell you more about peace."

"Please do."

"Peace," the deer continued, "is not just the absence of conflict. It is another way of relating to the world. Many men see themselves as men of peace who are really motivated by a fear of conflict rather than by a

real understanding of the true nature of peace. To be a true man of peace
you must choose peace, not out of fear of conflict but out of a commitment to follow another path. A warrior can choose to become a man of
peace. If he does, he must replace some of the warrior's principles with
other principles. Refusing to fight is not enough. A warrior who refuses
to fight is still a warrior. A warrior who chooses to become a man of
peace is no longer a warrior. The way of peace is powerful, just as
powerful as the way of the warrior, but it is different. The way of the deer
is as powerful as the way of the mountain lion, but we use our power
in different ways."

"How do I become a man of peace?" I asked.

"You can learn this best from the animals who are animals of peace.
The animals can tell you about how to live in peace but, more impor-
tantly, they can show you by allowing you to become one of them.
Yesterday you started to become a deer. You had some experience of
what it is like to be a deer. Do you remember that?"

"Yes."

"Do you remember the feeling of power that you had as an animal of
peace when you started to become a deer?"

"Yes, I do. It was a different feeling than I have ever had before. I knew
what it was like to be powerful and peaceful at the same time. I liked that
feeling. But I don't know how to be powerful and peaceful at the same
time as a man."

"Allow yourself to become an animal of peace more fully and you will
be able to be a man of peace when you choose. Allow yourself to become
a deer with regularity. Do the dance of the deer, meditate upon the deer
or talk to a deer, as you are doing now. Each of those three ways can
make you open to being changed into a deer. When you sense that you
are open, allow the change to occur. It is that simple. You started to
experience it yesterday. If you had been more open, the change would
have been more complete. When you are able to become a deer fully you
will be able to become a man of peace fully. There are other ways to
become a man of peace than through becoming an animal, but I do not
know those ways. I can only teach you what I know."

"I don't feel as if I am becoming a deer today. Why did it happen
yesterday but not today?"

Yesterday you were ready for it to happen, though you did not know
it; today you are not. It is not automatic. The animal will not overpower
you and make you change. You must be open for it to happen. You must,

on some level of your being, will for it to happen. Today you do not will it. That is all right; when you do, it will happen."

I sensed that we were finished for the day. A moment later the animal turned its head and moved off slowly through the undergrowth.

⚜ 6 ⚜

When I saw Flying Eagle I told him about my second experience with the deer and what the deer had said to me.

"The deer," mused Flying Eagle, "came to you before you came to him. That is very unusual. It is also unusual for an animal to talk with a person two days in a row. It means that the animal likes you. That is very important. When an animal talks to a person it can sense the nature of the person's heart. The animal likes your heart. Star Man is right; your heart is good."

"Even though I didn't eat all my spinach as a kid?" I asked jokingly.

Flying Eagle looked puzzled. He didn't seem to understand my attempt at humor.

"Maybe Indian mothers don't make their kids eat all their spinach," I mumbled. "Never mind. I guess it's a White Man's joke."

"Oh," he said and smiled, patiently.

"What do you mean, my heart is good?" I asked seriously. "I don't feel as though I'm an example of any unusually saintly qualities."

"The trouble with you," he said, "is that you think you know what words mean. You think that because you use the word 'good' that you know what it means and that you know what I mean by it. Goodness is not what you think it is. It is not, as you say, eating your spinach when you are supposed to. Many people think that religion is about being good in that sense, about following all the rules in life. But religion is not truly about that at all. The religion of my people is not about that and neither is yours. The missionary I told you about didn't understand that.

"Religion is about having a heart that is good. Goodness is not in obeying the rules. Goodness is about discovering that the Spirit lives within you and that you can live out the meaning of your life. You, my friend, never paid much attention to the rules but you do listen to the Spirit inside you and try to live true to its voice. That is very different from obeying the rules. That can even cause a person to get in trouble because, at times, he may do things differently than he was taught to do them by his society. In your religion Jesus is considered to have had a good heart but he got in trouble because he did not follow the rules of his religion. The rules are not what religion is all about; in fact, the rules are there only for guidance when people can not hear the voice of the Spirit within them. You hear the Spirit and try to follow it. That is why your heart is good."

"But if that is true why do religions have so many rules and regulations and rituals?"

"The rules and regulations are there, as I said, to guide people during the times when they can not hear their own inner voice. The rituals, however, have a different purpose. The rituals are tools that can be used to enter the world of the Spirit. There are many kinds of rituals in my religion. Your religion has some too. They are not important in themselves. They are only important as tools to get in touch with the realm of the Spirit. Some people try to make the rituals into rules and regulations. They say that one must do this or that ritual or, as the missionary told me, that one must go to church. That is not necessary. No ritual is necessary, but the rituals can be very helpful. For those who want to hear the voice of the Spirit more clearly the rituals can open the way. For those who are not truly interested in hearing the voice of the Spirit the rituals are an end in themselves, appreciated only for their beauty or pageantry. You must learn to hear the Spirit speaking in the silence between the words and actions of the rituals. Do you understand?"

"Yes, I think so. So all that going to church I did as a kid wasn't really important after all."

"Just being present at the services wasn't important but learning to use the tools of the Spirit world is very important. Did you hear the voice of the Spirit when you did the rituals?"

"Not very often. There were a few times that I felt really close to God, but most of the time I just felt bored. I went to church because my parents made me and because they said it was important."

"It is important to do the rituals, but not for the reasons that most people do them. Most people do them to get to something that is already there. They just don't know that the Spirit is already there. They think that they will get into the presence of the Spirit through the rituals. The Spirit is not present in the rituals. The Spirit is present through the rituals. The Spirit is within. You need to look within, in the midst of doing the rituals. Most people look to the Spirit to come to them. The

Spirit doesn't come. The Spirit is. It sounds to me as if you expected the Spirit to come to you in church and when you didn't experience the Spirit there, you decided that it was a waste of time. It is not the purpose of the rituals to bring anything to you. Their purpose is to open a pathway that you can follow to enter within. Without that element of entering within, the rituals are empty. I don't know why religions don't make that more clear to people. There are many Indians who do not understand that either.

"When you talked to the animal you could hear the animal's voice because you went within. The animal spoke but you could only hear it because you got in touch with the part of yourself that is a deer. People have many parts, many different animal ways within them. When you talk to the animals you are talking to the parts within yourself that understand the ways of the animals. The animal speaks and you hear it; that is true. But it is also true that you have spoken to the animal within you, not the animal outside of you. Both are true at the same time. But that is also true when you speak to another person using your voice. You are speaking to the voice of that person within you. It seems to you that the person is outside you and that you are talking to him or her out there. You are not; you are talking to what that person represents within you. When you don't like a person or don't like what a person is saying to you it is really that you don't like the part within you that that person represents. A man of peace knows that. That is why a man of peace does not kill his enemies. The man of peace knows that our enemies are really inside us and that killing people is a waste of time. The warrior fights evil in others but the true warrior also knows that the battle is really within himself. He knows that killing all his enemies does not ultimately solve the problem of evil."

"Are you saying that the warrior and the man of peace are following a similar path?"

"Yes. The true warrior fights an enemy outside himself but knows that the true enemy is within himself. The true man of peace fights the enemy within in order to deal with the enemy outside of himself. You want to be a man of peace but there is still much that you do not understand about being a man of peace. For you to understand fully what it means to be a man of peace you need to become a warrior."

"But I don't want to kill anybody."

"You don't have to kill people to be a warrior. Some warriors do kill people, but not all warriors kill. Being a warrior means fighting evil outside oneself in order to deal with the evil inside oneself. That is the nature of the true warrior. You, my friend, see the evil that is within you but you do not see it clearly. Some things that you think are evil about you, like not following some of the rules, are not evil. But other things that really do stand in the way of your hearing the voice of the Spirit you fail to recognize in yourself. For you to see yourself clearly you will need to become a warrior and deal with the evil that you see in others. Then you will be able to see yourself clearly. You are naive now. You can not see evil in others clearly. You keep trying to make others better than they are for fear that you will not be able to like them if you see them as they truly are. The command in your religion to love your enemy is a command designed for the warrior rather than for the man of peace. It is the warrior who is capable of seeing the evil in others clearly. When the warrior sees the evil and learns to accept that same evil as being within himself, he learns to love himself. You do not love yourself. You can only accept those parts of yourself that you think are good. You do not yet understand that all parts of you are good, even the parts that are evil. The true warrior comes face to face with that reality when he comes to love his enemies. Do you understand?

"No. I'm really confused. Sometimes you talk as though other people exist and then you talk as though they don't really exist. You talk as though evil exists and then you say that even evil is good. Which is true?"

"Both are true. Both are true at the same time. Until you can listen between the words you will not understand that, because the words sound like a contradiction to you. In the realm of the Spirit opposites can be true at the same time and usually are."

7

I went to the woods for the next three days. It was peaceful and relatively quiet. No animals came to me, but I enjoyed the time to process some of the things Flying Eagle had told me. His statement that opposites can be true at the same time kept running through my mind. It was confusing and yet, at the same time, it seemed to make sense. I thought about that a long time. Perhaps the world was not the way it seemed to be at all. Could it be that things I thought were absolutes were only one expression of an opposite truth? If that were true then death and life could exist simultaneously without conflict and without either one destroying the reality of the other. I remembered a funeral I had attended once where the family seemed deep in grief and yet appeared to be genuinely celebrating the entrance of the old man into the "larger life" at the same time. It struck me as strange at the time but it now started to make sense. Perhaps they were experiencing the reality of death and of resurrection simultaneously. If death and life are like that, could it possibly be that everything is like that? The thought got too big for me and started to scramble my brains. I decided to put it aside for a while and ask Flying Eagle about it when I got a chance.

A few days later the opportunity came. Flying Eagle had invited me to go along with him on one of his walks in the forest. We were walking and talking casually when the issue of the opposites returned to my mind and I decided to ask him about it.

"Flying Eagle, you said a few days ago that in the realm of the Spirit opposites can exist at the same time and usually do. What about the physical realm? Does the same rule apply in the physical realm?"

He stopped abruptly and looked at me hard and long. "Who spoke of this to you?" he asked.

I was surprised by the intensity of his reaction. "Nobody," I said. "I was just thinking the other day about what you said regarding the spirit realm and then I thought about the issue of death and resurrection. I just wondered if the coexistence of opposites was a rule that applies in the physical realm as well.

"Star Man taught me about that," he said solemnly. "No other person has ever talked to me about that before."

I got the definite impression that I had stumbled onto a subject that was far more important than I knew.

"Did I say something wrong?"

"No. Your question just surprised me, that's all. No one told you to ask that question?"

"No. As I said, it occurred to me when I was thinking about what you said regarding opposites in the realm of the Spirit. It seemed to be a natural progression from what you said."

Flying Eagle looked at me again as though he was choosing his words carefully and debating at the same time whether or not to say anything at all. Finally he said, "You have just asked me about the central issue on which all my power as a medicine man is based. I have not talked openly about it with anyone. Star Man told me about it but I have never discussed it with anyone else. Now you are asking me to tell you about it as though it were any other subject that you are curious about." He walked on in silence for a few minutes and then said. "Are you sure no one told you to ask me about this?"

"Yes, I'm sure," I said, feeling rather irritated at being asked the same question repeatedly. "Don't you believe me?"

"A medicine man does not talk about the source of his powers with just anyone. It is too dangerous. If an enemy found out the source of my powers he could use the information against me and bring great harm to my people."

I wasn't sure what to make of his response. The subject of evil had reared its ugly head again and this time it was beginning to sound to me like a line from the next Stephen King novel. "What do you mean?" I finally asked.

"You don't understand the importance of your question. If I tell you about the opposites in the physical realm and you understand it, you will have great powers for good or for evil. I'm not sure you are ready to know these truths. There are people who would use those powers for evil and would enhance their own sense of importance by manipulating things that they should leave alone. I am not sure you are ready to know the truth about this subject."

"Will you tell me about it when you think I am ready?"

"Yes, I will. I must. Star Man told me to tell you everything. But you are not ready now."

We finished our walk in silence and returned to the village.

≈ 8 ≈

Over the next few days I thought repeatedly about the intensity of Flying Eagle's reaction to my expressed desire for more knowledge about the opposites. It reminded me of the intensity of God's reaction to Adam and Eve eating the fruit and gaining the knowledge of good and evil. Can certain areas of knowledge truly be dangerous? I wondered. But I decided to leave the subject of the opposites alone, at least for a while.

Flying Eagle and I continued to meet over the next days. We talked about a variety of things. He did not bring up the opposites and neither did I. Then one day he said, "I want you to understand something. The opposites are not related to each other in the way that you suppose. Some things that appear to be radically different from each other are actually the same. Good and Evil appear to be opposites, but they are opposites that are the same."

I did not understand. But before I could ask him a question, he continued.

"And the power of the opposites is not a kind of magical power that the medicine man uses; it is the force of the universe that the medicine man learns how to channel. The discovery about the way opposites interact is the discovery of the way things really are. The rest is illusion. People live most of their lives in the illusion that things are the way they appear to be. Things are not the way they appear. The medicine man knows this and it is this knowledge that gives him his powers. The medicine man does not manipulate reality; he works with reality. He deals with the world the way it really is.

"Most people manipulate illusion as though it were reality. The rich man acts as though his riches had some importance and others also act as though his riches are important. But riches are not important. The importance of riches is an illusion. The medicine man knows that riches have no value. He also knows that the difference between good and evil is an illusion. Most people act as if some things are good and other things are bad, and as if there is virtue in doing what is good. The knowledge of good and evil is the knowledge that the two are the same; that it is the condition of one's heart that determines the nature of the world one lives in. To the person with a good heart all things are good. There are still choices to be made but they are not choices between good and evil; they are choices between what is desired and what is not desired. The person who does not have a good heart does not understand this and to him everything is bad. Your own religion teaches this. The Bible says that, 'in everything God works for good with those who love him, who are called according to his purpose.' That truth is in your religion but it is also in ours. The secret about good and evil is that they are the same."

"But you referred to some people as having good hearts while others do not have good hearts. Isn't that an acknowledgement of the existence of good and evil?"

"No, it is not. Creation just is; things are not good or evil. There is an appearance of good and evil but that is created by the individual. A person creates his own reality. A person whose heart is good creates a good universe. A person who does not have a good heart creates an evil universe out of the same substance. The substance is by nature neither good nor evil. Good and evil are the same.

"But why then is there so much talk about the Devil in my religion?"

"We have that concept too, but it is not because evil exists apart from us. Evil exists within us. Do you understand?"

"I think I am starting to. You mean that we have created the Devil just as we can create an evil universe out of what just is?"

"That's right." He beamed at me. "You understand. I am pleased."

"But why do you say that this knowledge is dangerous?"

"It is dangerous because it gives people the power to create. When people know that they have the power to make things good or evil there is the strong temptation to use this knowledge for selfish gain instead of furthering the purposes of the Spirit."

"But you just used the word selfish as though it were evil. Can selfishness be good?"

"Of course. When a person uses his awareness of his own needs as a source of information and aligns with the will of the Spirit, that person can create good for himself out of what is. All things can work together for good. But a person who only wants what he wants and cares nothing about the will of the Spirit does not create good; he creates evil. In order for a person to be able to use his creative power positively, he must be willing to serve the Spirit and to live a life of service to others."

"That sounds like Christianity."

"I have read your Bible. Much of what it says I know to be true about the Spirit. Our religions share many of the same truths. Religions come about partly as an attempt to express that which cannot truly be put into words. Religions try to deal with the way things really are. But to truly understand, you must be able to listen between the words. There is no other way. Your religion explains many things very well but you still must have faith or it is just words. A person without faith cannot listen between the words. The Spirit speaks to the person who has faith."

"You would make a good Christian," I said.

"I know." He paused and then said, "And by the way, I take that as a compliment. But my religion speaks of some things more clearly than yours. You are here to learn those things and I am here to teach you."

❧ 9 ❧

For the next week I did not see Flying Eagle. The meeting hall in the village was in need of repair and I volunteered to help the men with the project. It turned out to be a more elaborate project than I expected and I was kept busy from morning until night for a solid week. I didn't have time to go to the forest or to think much about what Flying Eagle had been teaching me. When we completed the final touches on the project, Flying Eagle came over to me and said, "What have you learned about the Spirit this week?"

"I've been busy all week. I haven't had time to think."

"So what have you learned about the Spirit this week?" he asked again.

"I've been busy with this project the entire time. I haven't had time to meditate or talk to you or walk in the forest or talk to the animals. I haven't had a minute to myself."

"I know," he said. "I told them to keep you occupied constantly. They did a good job of it.

"So tell me, what did you learn about the Spirit this week?"

I was feeling exasperated. By now I knew him well enough to know that he was coming to some point but I was tired and frustrated and just wanted him to get on with it.

"The trouble with White Men is that you think that work is important. Work is not important. Doing things is not important. Accomplishing things is not important. You thought that your work was so important that you could not learn about the Spirit this week. You do not understand. If you think that your work is important you will not be able to hear the voice of the Spirit when you are working. It is only when you know that your work is not important that you will be able to work and to learn at the same time."

"But I don't understand how I can learn about the Spirit when I am so busy."

"There is a difference between being active and being busy. You are busy because you think that your work is important. A busy man cannot learn. But a person can be active and still learn. When a person does things knowing that they are unimportant he is active but not busy. Most White Men are busy. You, my friend, were very busy and that is why you did not learn. You think that what you do has something to say about who you are, that your identity is related to what you accomplish; so you stay busy. But being busy does nothing for a person and says nothing about a person other than that he does not yet know that work is not important."

"The other men on that job looked just as busy as I was. Were they?"

"Some were busy like you but others were active. It is hard to tell the difference unless you know their hearts. While we have been talking you have forgotten that your work is important and so you have started learning again."

"You are right. Talking to you and learning what you have to teach me is all that seems important at this moment."

"So you have learned that your work is not important. It is easier to know that when you are not working than it is when you are in the midst of a project. To be working and to know at the same time that your work is not important; that is important." He chuckled softly to himself and walked off.

I sat down, wiped the sweat off my brow and then headed off to the showers knowing that that too was not important.

≈10≈

Some of Flying Eagle's teachings seemed strange at first, even mind boggling, but with time they seemed more and more to be rather natural descriptions of the way things really are as opposed to the way things appear to be. My stay in the village had caused me to do some deep thinking about my life and about the meaning that I had ascribed in the past to things that now seemed unimportant. I thought about how much of my time and energy had been tied up with jobs or special projects and how unimportant they all seemed now in retrospect. Most of my life I had been busy instead of just being active. But my thoughts about all this were interrupted by Flying Eagle's arrival.

"It is time," he announced, "for you to learn to be a warrior."

"I'm still not sure I want to become a warrior," I said, feeling a bit off balance by this sudden shift of focus.

"That does not matter. It is time."

We went for another walk in the forest. "Being a warrior is not what you think it is. It is about learning how to use your own power. You are a victim of life much of the time. The warrior is not a victim. The warrior encounters life and changes what is not suitable. The warrior encounters the evil in himself and prevails. You do not want to be a warrior because you think that you will be changed into that which you do not like. You are already that which you do not like. You already have a warrior within you. I am not asking you to become something different; I am asking you to let that which is already inside you be fully expressed. When you express the warrior, you will have new freedom to be either a warrior or a man or peace. The warrior and the man of peace are similar; they both contend with evil. But you don't like to contend with evil; you like to ignore it. As long as you ignore it, it will have power over you. The warrior gains his power through confronting evil. It is the conflict with evil that empowers the warrior.

"But I don't want to fight. I want to bring peace."

"You don't have any power to bring peace. You are a man with no power. It is as the warrior fights evil that he discovers his own power. You do not know your own power because you try to ignore evil and pretend that it is not there. You rob yourself of power when you do that because you are not empowered by the conflict."

"Wait a minute. I thought you said before that nothing is evil or good, that things just are. If we create the meaning; if we create evil, then why is it important to fight evil."

"Because evil exists. It is true that evil exists only because you have created it out of what is, but it does exist; and, if you ignore what exists, you will rob yourself of power. Power comes from dealing with things the way they really are; and it comes from recognizing evil and contending against it. Evil is created by you but once it is created it is real and must be dealt with as a reality. If you ignore evil you are ignoring reality."

"I don't like this subject," I said honestly. "It gives me the creeps. And I have never liked the kind of people who go around talking about evil all the time."

"A person can get out of balance and focus too much on evil. That is not helpful, but you focus too little on evil. That is dangerous. It is time for you to experience evil."

We took another walk through the forest. He led me up a hill, perhaps a hundred feet high, that had a small clearing on top of it. In the center of the clearing was an area with a small circle of rocks that had obviously been a fire place in the past.

"I want you to gather enough wood to keep a fire going through the night. Place the wood near the fire circle so you can reach it from where you will be sitting in front of the fire. You will spend tonight in front of this fire. You are not to let the fire go out tonight and you are not under any circumstances to leave the fire circle tonight." Having said that, he sat down on a rock and waited while I gathered the fire wood. When I had completed the pile, he led me back through the forest in silence. When we arrived at the village, he finished his instructions.

"Return to the hill tonight at sundown. Light the fire and remain there until sunrise. Do not leave the fire. You will have an encounter with evil tonight. Remember, whatever happens, do not leave. If you do, you will be in great danger." Before I could respond, he turned abruptly and walked away.

≈ 11 ≋

The sun was about to go down when I reached the clearing at the top of the hill. I quickly laid the fire and started it. Then I sat down to wait. This time I was not sure what it was I was waiting for. Flying Eagle said that I would have an encounter with evil but what form would that take? Was I waiting for an animal, waiting for Flying Eagle, waiting for some ghoulish monster? I didn't know.

Time passed. I thought about various manifestations of evil in the world; war, torture, the holocaust. I remembered with revulsion the sheer delight I once heard in a pilot's voice as he described enemy foot soldiers running in stark terror as he gunned them down.

"Evil," I thought, "evil exists because I have created it? How can that be? Did I create that pilot who enjoyed destroying human life? Did I create the holocaust?"

The evening wore on. I put more wood on the fire. I sat and continued to ponder. I thought about how much I valued peace, tranquillity and the brother and sisterhood of all people. I stood for what was good and decent and right. I could never knowingly be involved in the taking of human life. Well, perhaps through ignorance or carelessness, but I could never take a human life out of choice. I could never knowingly destroy that which I considered sacred.

Then it happened. A figure appeared silently and stood between me and the fire, blocking its warmth. I was surprised but not frightened. There was something familiar about the presence, something familiar and yet also unknown.

"You do not know your heart," my visitor said flatly. "You don't know why you returned, do you? You don't have any idea why you returned." There was a sneering quality to his voice. My initial feeling of comfort with my visitor rapidly shifted to anxiety. "You think you value peace? You think you stand for what is good and noble and right?

"You are so good! So brave! So noble to meet me here by the fire. Do you have any idea who I am?"

His face was in shadows.

"No," I said, "but for some reason you look familiar. Have we met before?"

"Many times, in many places. I am part of you. And I am here to help you remember things that you have forgotten."

"Remember what things?" I asked and then immediately regretted my question. Something within told me that I didn't want an answer. I had a sudden impulse to run. I wanted to get away from whatever was coming next.

"No, No, No," he taunted. "You want to run away from yourself? That would be very dangerous. I am here to help you meet yourself." His voice became vicious. "To help you meet yourself and remember!"

Suddenly, I could feel myself on a horse, a strong, powerful horse. And then I could see it. I was there riding across rolling grassy hills. It was hot. The sun was beating down on me but it felt good on my back and I enjoyed the sensation of the sweat running down between my shoulder blades under my blue uniform. I felt strong. I felt powerful. I felt in charge of my life.

I raised my arm to shield my eyes as I rode over the crest of a hill. And then I saw what I had been looking for. In the distance was a cluster of tepees, fifteen, maybe twenty of them pitched beside a small stream.

I quickly dismounted and led my horse back behind the hill, out of sight or the village. Then I returned to the top of the hill, crawling the last part of the way on all fours. I crouched in the gently waving grass and watched.

I felt excited. I could see small figures moving back and forth among the tepees, inhabitants tending to their chores. I saw no signs of alarm. The figures moved slowly. Apparently I had not been seen. I could feel a smile spreading across my face.

I watched carefully for another minute and then crawled back over the crest of the hill, ran to my horse and galloped back to a column of blue coated cavalry.

I reigned my horse to a stop in front of the lieutenant and said breathlessly, "They're there, Sir! They're camped upstream. I didn't see any horses in the village. I think the men are away hunting buffalo. We can take 'em, Sir."

"Did they see you?"

"No Sir, I don't think so."

"Good work."

The lieutenant started shouting orders.

The next thing I saw was the village in total disarray. Bodies were scattered around the still-burning fires and we were picking our way back through the village looking for any remaining signs of life.

I was still on my horse. There was fresh blood on my sword. I felt exhilarated.

Then I saw a young child, almost a baby, lying next to its dead mother. It was making a whimpering sound. As I drew close, our eyes met. There were tears streaming down its face and a look of bewildered terror in its eyes as it clutched its dead mother for comfort. It was then that the full impact of what I had been a part of hit me. The excitement vanished. I was horrified. I felt sick. I vomited. The scene ended.

The figure in front of me spoke. "Do you remember now?" he sneered.

I was too shaken to speak. Finally my voice returned and I asked haltingly, "Was I that soldier?"

"Yes, you were, we were. I am a part of you."

"But I hate fighting. I hate cruelty. And I hate people who do such things. I'm appalled by what I saw. How could that have been me?"

"Now that you have seen it. You hate what you were. But you are still what you were. Now you are afraid of that violent nature of yours. You run from it. And you consider yourself a man of peace? You don't understand the ways of peace and you still don't understand what it is to be a warrior. You didn't learn it then. You haven't learned it yet. And you really think you can learn it now?" My visitor laughed. "You have come back to try again. You really fell for it the last time! You thought that just being violent would make you a warrior, didn't you? And this time you think that just running away from violence will make you a man of peace. You still don't get it! You are here to do battle with yourself."

The presence vanished.

For the rest of the night I sat alone by the fire. Fresh memories of the massacre raced through my head. I felt numb. I felt frightened. I wanted to run, to scream, to escape from myself. But I couldn't move. I was frozen by the image of that child, looking up at me. He saw what I had done. He saw me as I really was and he was terrified.

Shortly after dawn I heard familiar footsteps approaching. I sat in silence as Flying Eagle came into the clearing and sat down beside me. He laid his hand on my shoulder. I was still shaking.

"How are you doing?" he asked softly.

I started to sob.

"Did you encounter evil?"

I nodded my head. "Yes," I whispered. Then haltingly I told him about my visitor and about what I had remembered.

"I can't believe that I could have been a part of anything so horrible. And yet, there is a part of me that knows, really knows, that I was there and that I did those things."

More waves of grief and shame engulfed me. We sat in silence. It hurt. It hurt more than any pain I had ever experienced before.

Finally the intensity of the pain started to subside.

"Flying Eagle, I was raised to believe that reincarnation is a bunch of bunk, but last night made a believer out of me."

"Well," he said slowly, "I don't believe in reincarnation." He paused and then added, "I used to, but that was in a former life." Then he roared with laughter.

In my troubled state it took me a few moments to catch the humor in his statement. Then I laughed too, but not as hard as Flying Eagle, who seemed totally delighted with himself.

"But really, Flying Eagle, how can you laugh about this. I'm serious."

He gave me a gentle squeeze around the shoulders with one arm and then said, still chuckling, "I know you are. I know you are.

"You'll have to forgive me. Sometimes the profundity of reality is very amusing. It amuses me that those who are in touch with their own evil are more open to the true goodness of the Spirit than those pursue goodness and think that they have attained it."

"What?"

"Oh, never mind, that will all make sense to you later, and then maybe it will be amusing to you too.

"Now, getting back to that issue of reincarnation," he said. "There are many people who can recall experiences they had during previous lifetimes. The memories are real. The experiences are real. The issues are real. But what they remember from a past life is affected by who they are now. What you remembered last night actually occurred. But you may not remember the events in a past life exactly the way they occurred in history. Your past is affected by who you are now. Your future and your past are not fixed, both can be changed. Who you are now can affect what happened to you in the past just as who you are now can affect what you will do in the future. This is very hard to explain. People are so accustomed to thinking of the past as being fixed, unchangeable. It is not. You encountered your past last night and your past showed you that, under a different set of circumstances, you are quite capable of destroying life. Memories of your past lives are not a totally reliable way to study historical events but they can be quite useful in helping you to understand who you are now. Is that clear?"

"Yes, but I don't like it. That memory means that I am still capable of being involved in a massacre."

"Yes, it does. Your circumstances are different now, but if you were placed back in the same conditions that existed during your former life you might do the same thing again. The evil that you thought was beyond you is still a part of who you are. Until you can see yourself in the atrocities committed by others you are not on the true path of the warrior. The warrior does not fight evil because he himself represents the forces of good. The warrior knows that he is in battle with an enemy who represents another part of himself. You create the evil you encounter and only you can change it."

"Does that mean that my memories of that massacre will change if I make changes in my life now?"

"Perhaps, but probably not. Once a memory from a past life has been fully recalled the memory itself becomes a part of that person's present life. Memories that have been fully recalled do not usually change even if the person changes. But other events that the person has not yet consciously recalled may be changed if the person makes changes in who he is now."

"I'm still confused by all this, Flying Eagle."

"You are and you will be, but that does not change the fact that it is time for breakfast. Let's go. I like you, but I'm not willing to miss my breakfast for you or anybody else."

I laughed. We stood up and headed back to the village together.

12

After breakfast I went to bed and slept most of the day. Late in the afternoon Flying Eagle stopped by my room to check on me.

"How are you feeling?" he asked when he saw that I was awake. He seemed to be genuinely concerned about my well being. Over the past days I had been growing genuinely fond of Flying Eagle as a person and I could tell that he was feeling closer to me as well. I was no longer just another student to him.

"Well, I had a little nightmare that I was being eaten alive by a hideous monster. Other than that I'm doing fine."

"Your dreams will return to normal in a few days. You are looking better now. This morning you looked a little pale."

"You might say that I didn't have a very pleasant night. I don't like what I learned about myself."

"But I am proud of you," he said. "It is not easy to face the evil that lies within us. Some run away. Some go into deep denial about what they have remembered, referring to it as an interesting or frightening dream. And some totally blot out what they are shown about themselves. You did not run and you are struggling to deal with what you have learned about yourself. I am proud of you."

"It's not easy. What I remembered scares me. I'd like to run away from it but I can't."

"You are brave. A brave man feels fear, but the brave man faces his fear and stays in spite of it. Facing the truth about oneself can be more frightening than facing an enemy in combat. I am proud of you." I could sense that he really meant that. "Now you have met the evil in yourself and you know that it exists. You have the courage necessary to become a warrior, but you must now learn how to contend against evil and prevail; only then can you choose to become a true man of peace with power."

"You still want me to become a warrior don't you? I'm still not sure that's what I want."

"That is because you don't realize its importance. Now that you have met the evil, and now that you know that you have returned to learn the way of the warrior, it is no longer safe for you to ignore its reality. If you do not learn how to contend with the evil within you, it will conquer you. Your life now depends on learning how to be a warrior. I will teach you."

He was offering me a choice between life and death. Whether that was literal or figurative I didn't know and didn't care. How could I choose death over life?

"All right," I said, "but just a little warrior, O.K.?" I held up my thumb and index finger with less than an inch separating them.

He laughed out loud and slapped me on the back. "A warrior is a warrior. You will be a warrior."

The die was cast; my journey had now begun anew. Like it or not, I was on the way to becoming a true warrior.

～ 13 ～

Flying Eagle started meeting with me more frequently and for longer periods of time. My decision to become a warrior was a real turning point for me. I was no longer learning simply to satisfy my curiosity. I was learning in order to become. Despite my lack of knowledge, Flying Eagle moved me from the category of student to colleague and friend. He now referred to me as Little Warrior and always used that term with a gentle smile on his face. I grew daily in both my admiration and love for him. He talked openly with me about his vulnerabilities and about the blocks he had encountered over the years in his quest for the Spirit. His areas of weakness became sources of strength in our relationship.

"You are a strange man, Little Warrior," he said one day. "You are not an Indian, and yet most of the time you seem to understand our ways with little effort. But at other times your ignorance and lack of understanding astounds me. We talk deeply about the Spirit and you seem to understand, but when we talk of the rituals you do not seem able to grasp that we are not primarily concerned about the physical result of the ritual; we are concerned with transformation. You understand some things so well but others don't get through your thick skull." He tapped me gently on the head.

"I have noticed that too," I said. "I'm not sure what the problem is. It's as though my brain keeps changing what you say to me about rituals into something else and then I get confused, not by what you have actually said but by the way I interpret what you have said."

"What do my words become in your mind?"

"They become explanations of how to manipulate reality. I know that is not what you are saying. You tell me that you are not manipulating reality through rituals, that you are merely dealing with reality as it truly is, but I keep hearing it as manipulation. The rain dance for example, I know it works; I've seen it work, but it seems like one big manipulation of Nature to get it to do what you want it to do."

"Little Warrior, nature is the action of the will of the Spirit. You do not understand how creation works and you do not understand the rain dance. You think you understand because you have seen the results. You think that the dance is about making it rain. It rains when we do the rain dance, but not for the reasons you suppose. It rains because it is the will of the Spirit. The dance is not to make it rain. The dance is to align our wills with the will of the Spirit. When that happens it rains. The Spirit creates and we create. The Spirit creates all that is. When our will is not in agreement with the Spirit's will, we create opposition to the Spirit; then things do not happen that would happen if we were not opposing the Spirit. It is the Spirit's will to water the earth. The Spirit takes care of her and meets her needs. When it does not rain it is because the will of the Spirit is being blocked. The Spirit allows this to happen because the Spirit has given us some of His power to create. The Spirit allows us to create and the Spirit allows us to block creation. When the will of the people is different from the will of the Spirit, the natural process of the Spirit's creation is stopped. The Spirit allows it to stop. The Spirit does not force His creation upon us. The Spirit only gives to us."

"You are saying then that the dance is not about making it rain as its first objective?"

"Yes. The dance is about aligning the will of the people with the will of the Spirit. When that happens it will rain because the will of the Spirit is then free to operate unopposed."

"But why would people want it not to rain if they and their crops and animals depend on the rain for water?"

"It is not that they do not want it to rain; it is that they are unconcerned about the will of the Spirit. When people start going in their own directions without concern about following the will of the Spirit or serving other people's needs, the rain stops. It is not that they want the rain to stop. It is that they want their will in all things above the will of the Spirit. When they want their own will above all else, then the Spirit allows His will to be blocked and the rain does not come. Many times people want the same things the Spirit wants but their self-absorption prevents the Spirit from acting. Do you understand now?"

"Yes, I think so. Then the rituals are not to manipulate nature; they are to allow nature to follow its natural course."

"That's right. That is what prayer is, but many people do not understand this. They think prayer is the process of convincing the Spirit to do what they want. It does not work that way. Prayer is first aligning oneself with the Spirit, then if one's will and the will of the Spirit are in agreement, the way is opened for what is willed to happen."

"But you said that the rituals are about transformation, not physical results. What did you mean?"

"Some rituals, like the rain dance, bring about physical results, others do not. But all rituals are designed to bring about transformation. Transformation occurs when the physical realm and the spiritual realm meet. Results are what happens in the physical realm. Results are unimportant. With regard to rain, it could rain only in the physical realm. Water could come from the sky, but the people might not receive it as a gift from the Spirit and might not be nurtured and strengthened by the giving of the water to the earth. The rain in that case is just a result. When it rains and the people receive it as a gift from the life giving Spirit, then the rain waters and gives life to the souls of the people as well. That is transformation because the event has had an impact on the physical realm and the spiritual realm at the same time. The purpose of the rituals is to bring about transformation rather than just results. Your culture seems to me to be mostly concerned about results. The rains come, money comes, success comes but the people are not nurtured by them. Your people remain dry and empty. Your people have forgotten the power of the rituals. They need to bring the physical realm and the spiritual realm into harmony. The rituals do that."

"But church services seem so empty to me most of the time. Aren't they rituals?"

"Your services where the physical and the spiritual are brought together are rituals. In your religion you use water and wine and bread in your transformation rituals. They can be powerful, but if people are only interested in themselves and are present at the services primarily to get something, then they are not open to the power of the rituals. Many people try to use the rituals to make the Spirit do what they want. They want the Spirit to become their servant. The Spirit gives to us freely, but we are not here to be served by the Spirit. We are here to serve the Spirit and to serve others. If we come to the rituals as servants we will experience great power; we will experience transformation rather than just empty results."

"I am learning more from you about the true nature of my own religion than I ever learned in church. Why is that?"

"Your people's understanding of your religion is incomplete. All the things that I have told you so far are in your religion already but you did not understand because many of your people have lost their vision.

My people have maintained an understanding of many of the things that are confusing to your people. We understand the rituals. We know how to care for the earth. We know many things about the Spirit. We are here to teach you but most of your people do not want to listen. That is why Star Man told me to teach you. He said that the White Man whose heart was good would be able to understand and would teach his people. I am teaching you and you must teach your own people."

14

I was feeling a sense of progress in my work with Flying Eagle. Despite the differences in our backgrounds what he had to say seemed to make sense of religious issues that had been confusing to me for years. I continued to be confused about Nature, however, and found that he consistently used that word in contexts that were foreign to me.

"Tell me about Nature," I said one afternoon as we watched billowing white clouds drifting over the mountain range in the distance. It was a gorgeous day, and it was hard not to be overwhelmed by the beauty of creation.

"To understand Nature is to understand the Creator," he said quite simply and stopped, as though he had just told me everything there was to know about the subject.

"But I already understand that, I think."

"You do not understand that. That is where your problem lies. If you understood that you would not be asking me about Nature."

"O.K., O.K., then I don't understand. Tell me about Nature, please."

He paused, took another one of his deep breaths and started speaking with a special reverence in his deep voice that I had not heard before. It was the tone that I imagine the high priest might have used as he stood alone before the Holy of Holies.

"Nature is the full expression of the will of the Spirit. In Nature we see the awesome love of the Creator revealed to us completely. The Creator is not the God of control and order that many think he is. He is the God of love and flexibility that is revealed in Nature.

"When the White Man looks at Nature he sees law and order, this event affecting that event and bringing about this or that result. When we look at Nature we see the love of the Creator expressed in an unending number of ways with great variety. The way that the animals live in the forest is not an expression of rigid rules of behavior; it is a demonstration of total freedom to experience and enjoy what is there.

The animals live in harmony with the natural order. Love brings harmony. Rules bring order. The animals do not live by rules. They live by harmony. It is the Creator's love for them and their love for the Creator that brings them into harmony with life.

"Your people do not understand this. Your people study Nature as though it could be broken down into rules. Then they try to use the rules to make Nature do what they want. You plant crops that are foreign to the land and then have to bring much water, fertilizers and pesticides to the land to keep your plants alive. You build dams to hold the water that you need and you kill the fish that live in the streams. You do not know how to live off what the land provides. You do not know how to live in harmony with Nature. You do not love Nature. Learning to use the rules only brings results. It does not bring transformation. Your people do not live in harmony with Nature; they do not love the earth and the sky and the seas; they do not allow Nature to meet all their needs as the animals do. If your people loved Nature they would live in harmony with Nature. They would know how to care for the earth."

"You talk about loving Nature almost like loving another person," I said. "How can you love an organizing force, a power, so personally?"

"But that is what you don't understand; Nature is like a person. It has will and feelings and love. If you treat Nature as if it does not have these things, you will never understand Nature. The first thing you must know about Nature is that it has no rules, only will and love. It is love that controls Nature and those who respond with love live in harmony with Nature.

"That is a different way to look at it," I said, still not convinced.

"You do not yet understand. You do not believe me. But you will. You will."

Somehow I didn't like the sound of that. It reminded me of my hard learned lesson about the reality of evil, a lesson I was not anxious to repeat.

"I just have trouble with thinking of Nature in such a personal way."

"That is because you do not understand that love is the power behind the universe and that it is always personal. Your own religion teaches that but you do not understand. Nature is love. It is love in action, but you do not yet understand that. You will. My words will not teach that to you, but you will come to understand."

I felt the vast difference between our cultures. I could not feel the way he did about Nature. My scientific mind could understand Nature as forces and cycles and patterns, but it could not understand it as love in action. It was then that he laid the really big one on me.

"I can tell that my words have not convinced you. Your problem is greater than just a problem with Nature. Little Warrior, despite all that your religion has taught you, you don't yet believe that God really is love."

I thought about it and realized that he was right.

"You do not yet believe it," he said, "but you will."

ॐ 15 ॐ

I still did not fully understand Nature, but I felt I had a better understanding of my lack of understanding. Flying Eagle said I did not believe that God is love. I seemed to have the same question about God that I had about Nature. How can one love an organizing force, a power? I wondered if that could be the problem. Perhaps God was more than a force or power in the universe. What if God did indeed have the personal qualities of will and feelings and love. The Bible certainly referred to God in those ways. I had always reinterpreted those passages and made God into an organizing force or principle. If God really does have will, feelings and love then maybe it is possible to love and be loved by God in a personal way. I puzzled over that one. My mind said, "Maybe." My heart said, "I don't know." The next time I met with Flying Eagle I brought it up with him.

"I'm still having trouble, with this concept of Nature and God as love. I understand it, but I don't grasp it, if you know what I mean."

"Your mind understands but your heart does not."

"That's right. I can think it but I can't feel it."

"That is not something that you are going to come to through your understanding. Truth is not in the words, remember? Your people usually depend on learning to bring them into relationship with the Spirit. That doesn't work. The truth is not in any words that can be learned. One must depend on experience."

He paused for a moment, then said, "It is time for you to meet Star Man. He came to me last night. We talked about you at great length. He said that you are ready. He will meet with you tonight."

I felt a twinge of excitement, butterflies in my stomach just as I had before my first school play. I was scared and excited. "Where will I meet him?" I asked, suddenly not knowing what else to say.

"You can meet him anywhere, but we agreed that he would come to you at the fire. Go there and gather firewood this afternoon. Then return there at sundown. You will meet him tonight." Flying Eagle smiled and walked away.

I immediately set off for the clearing. I gathered the fire wood and returned to the village.

The rest of the day passed slowly. I was restless, nervous and jittery. I thought about what I wanted to ask Star Man. I made lists of questions, then tore them up, then wrote them out again. I tried to take a nap so I would be rested for the night ahead. I slept fitfully. The afternoon dragged on. Finally it was time to go to the clearing.

I entered the forest and followed the trail to the clearing. The memory of my encounter with evil in that clearing was still fresh. The fear returned, but I pressed on. As the sun sank behind the mountain I lit the fire and prepared for the evening.

I waited. Late in the evening I heard a few soft footsteps coming from out of the darkness and then he was there, with me by the fire. He was as Flying Eagle had described him. He was dressed in plain Indian buckskins and moccasins. His hair sparkled and he wore one silver feather in his head band.

Despite all of my preparation for the encounter, I did not know what to say. We sat in silence. Finally he spoke.

"You have come to learn about the Spirit," he said. His voice had a beautiful quality to it, not feminine, but beautifully masculine and deep. Just the sound of his voice was moving, like listening to a great Shakespearean actor.

"You have asked the central question about love. I am here to teach you. You have prepared many questions. We will not deal with them now. Some of them Flying Eagle will answer for you, others we will deal with at a later time. Tonight we will deal with only one question. The one about love. One must answer that question before fully entering into the realm of the Spirit."

We sat in silence again. The silence had a quality to it that I find hard to describe. It was productive, active silence. Although I had no new insights during these periods without conversation, internal work seemed to be going on at a level deeper than words.

The fire gradually died down. He reached over and put some wood on it. Then he continued. "You think love is something that it is not. You identify love with your feelings. Because of that you think love is a feeling. It is not."

Again we sat in active silence. Then, "You do not understand that love is commitment. That love is profound commitment not with the mind but with the heart. You do not love with the mind. You love with the heart, but you do not feel with the heart. Love is on a deeper level than feelings. You can not always detect it with your feelings. That has caused much confusion for your people. They think that they must feel something when love is encountered. Sometimes they do. Sometimes they do not. Your people do not understand that love is a dimension like time or space. It is what is. Love is what is. It is behind all creation. Creation came forth out of that dimension. Creation expresses love but is not itself love; it is love put into action."

He paused again. The silence was powerful.

"Love is what is," he continued. "Love is the deepest dimension. You do not create it. Because you feel things that you associate with love, you think that it is your love. You can not create love within yourself. You can create some things but you can not create love. In its purest form it is encountered on the level of silence. Beneath matter and energy and all things that can be encountered in the physical or spiritual realm is love. Love is the basic element behind all that is."

We sat in profound silence again. Finally I spoke. "But what you are saying sounds so impersonal."

"That is because you do not yet understand," he said.

He was right. I did not understand.

"When love comes in its purest form people do not recognize it because they are expecting it to be something else. It has always been that way and it is that way with you. Love comes and you do not recognize it. You keep trying to make it into that which it is not. You want love to feel good. Sometimes it does; sometimes it doesn't. You want love to make you feel good about yourself, but sometimes it reveals things that you do not like about yourself. Love always draws one back, into deeper levels of oneself, toward one's beginnings or onward, into new areas, toward one's end. Love is the beginning and the end. Love is the essence out of which all things come and toward which all things go. It is the elemental essence of the universe. As you encounter it you are changed; you must be changed; for love is constantly in transition and yet always the same."

My head was swimming. I couldn't take it all in. "I can't understand all of that. It's too much, too fast."

"You will not understand it all now, but you will. You will remember my words and you will come to understand them all in time.

"There is but a little more that I will tell you tonight about love. You have encountered evil. You now know it to be real. The evil that you encountered was the evil that you yourself created. But there are times when you will encounter the evil created by others. When that happens you will be presented with four options. You can choose to ignore evil, or to run from it, or to define its boundaries or to suffer its effects willingly. If you ignore it or make no choice at all you will become its victim. If you run from it you make yourself vulnerable to attack and it may choose to attack you. If you, as a warrior, define and then defend its boundaries, you will limit its effects. If you take the fourth option and choose willingly to suffer its effects, you can change its power into good. Few choose to suffer its effects willingly. But those who do, change the world. The fourth option is about love and can only come about through love. The fourth option is the most powerful of all.

"Remember what I have told you. Remember the words. But remember also that the truth is not in the words themselves; it is in the silence between the words. In the silence love speaks."

There was another long period of silence. Then he stood up and turned toward me. I stood up facing him. He spoke again. "I will go but I am here," he said. "Remember, love is not what you think it is.

"Peace be with you." As he said that, he raised his hand in the classic Indian gesture. The sleeve of his buckskins slipped away from his hand and I could see a deep, ugly wound in the palm of his hand just above his wrist.

"My God!" I gasped. "Who are you?" I demanded.

But he had disappeared.

℀ 16 ℁

I was still sitting by the fire in stunned silence when dawn broke across the sky in blazing color. I put out what remained of the glowing embers and started walking slowly back to the village. When I reached the base of the hill I saw Flying Eagle walking briskly toward me like a man in his 20's.

"Good morning!" he boomed. "How was your night in the forest?"

I still felt in a state of shock. "I'm still trying to absorb what happened. His hand, the wound in his hand...."

Flying Eagle looked deep into my eyes and smiled tenderly. "You know the secret; don't you? He said he was going to show you his wounds. I thought it was too soon, but he said that you were ready."

"Star Man is Jesus, isn't he."

"Yes." He put his hand on my shoulder and we walked slowly back toward the village together. "He does not show his wounds to everyone, only to a few. It was on his third visit to me that he showed them to me. At first I didn't understand. It took me a few days. Then it hit me. Our religions are the same. What we know about Nature you are supposed to learn from us. What you know about forgiveness we are supposed to learn from you. It is the same Spirit and we are brothers. I tried to tell that to the missionary when he came. He would not listen. He kept trying to tell me about Jesus. I kept telling him that I already knew Jesus, but he wouldn't listen. He talked about church and leaving our pagan ways and becoming like him. I did not want to become like him. I had experienced Jesus in the forest by the fire. I had talked to him. He had spoken to me in my own language and taught me about the Spirit and the true meaning of our rituals. The missionary wanted me to leave all that and follow a Jesus that he had only heard about. I could not make him understand. But I believe that you understand. Now you have met Star Man and you know his other name."

"He taught me about love," I said. "I didn't understand a lot of what he told me. I got confused and couldn't take it all in."

"It was many years, "Little Warrior," before I understood all that he taught me about love. He told me that love was not what I thought it was. He said that I had been seeking the Spirit because I wanted the Spirit to serve me, to meet my needs, to answer my prayers, to give me wisdom and knowledge. He said that I would not learn the true meaning of love until I was willing to give up my desire to be served and was willing to die for my people. That seemed ridiculous to me. I did not want to serve a Spirit who asked that of me. It didn't make sense. But slowly it did start to make sense and I discovered that he was right. I had not known what love was at all. I had only thought that I knew what love was. He had told me that love was not a feeling but I had not believed him. I had not wanted to believe him. I wanted love to make me feel good. He told me that love would empower me to be able to give up my life for others. I had not wanted that. But gradually I came to understand and you will too. I wanted to be the center of my own life and my own little universe, but we are not the center of the universe. Love is. When I stopped looking for love to serve me, to meet my needs, to make me feel good, I discovered its true nature. Love is not as pretty as it used to be for me, but it is far more wonderful."

"Flying Eagle, what keeps going through my head is that wound. When I learned as a kid that Jesus died in the way that he did because he loved people, I automatically thought that meant that he had the tender feeling for people that I call love. Somehow seeing the wound destroyed that for me. The wound made it all very real. I can no longer picture a man hanging from that kind of a real wound because he feels a warm glow for people. If his death was about love then love has to be something more real and more powerful than a warm feeling."

"You are beginning to understand," he said simply. "The wounds are the key to understanding what love really is. Keep thinking about them. See what emerges. We will talk more later."

We had reached the village. He left me at the dining hall. I ate a quick breakfast, returned to my room and lay down. But I couldn't sleep. I kept thinking about the wounds. When Jesus appeared to his disciples after the crucifixion he showed them his wounds. Could it have been more than just a way to prove to them who he was? When I saw the wound I recognized him as Jesus but seeing the wound also started to shift my perception of the true nature of love. I had always relied on recognizing love through a feeling. Suddenly I was recognizing love in an ugly, gaping wound. I could no longer go back to thinking of love as a feeling.

Around noon I finally fell into a deep sleep.

17

I awakened with a start. It was late in the afternoon. I had been dreaming. In my dream there was a wound in a man's hand. As I approached, it opened wider and wider until it became a great cavern. I reached the mouth of the wound and then started screaming, "No! No!" and clawing wildly for a grip on anything that could keep me from being drawn inside. Despite all my resistance, I was pulled into the wound by some unseen force and found myself in total darkness. I could not see, hear or feel anything. Then a cup was thrust into my hands from somewhere in the darkness. I took a drink from the cup and was instantly ejected from the cave onto a beautiful sunny meadow with birds and flowers and gentle breezes rippling through the tall grass. I walked through the meadow for a while enjoying its beauty and then found myself being drawn back to the mouth of the ugly wound again and pulled inside. The cycle repeated itself three times in all before the dream ended with me sobbing at the base of large dead tree in the midst of the meadow.

"A Freudian would have a lot of fun with that dream," I said to myself.

I tried to go back to sleep but couldn't get the dream out of my mind. Finally I got up and wrote it down. Just as I had finished writing I heard a gentle, barely audible, tap at my door. It was Flying Eagle. I invited him in.

"I heard your spirit calling to me," he said. "Are you all right?"

"I think so," I said and then told him about my dream.

"Your dream is very important," he said. "It is a spirit dream, about the nature of your spirit. I had one also after I met Star Man for the first time. Mine was different from yours, but it too was a spirit dream."

"What does it mean?" I asked.

"The Spirit communicates with your spirit. The Spirit teaches your spirit how to fulfill your mission in life. There are many ways that this can be done; there is no one path, but there is one way that is better for you than others at this time. The dream comes to reveal that path to you. Your spirit understands the dream even though your mind does not. It is as though your spirit has received a private set of instructions from the Great Spirit, instructions that it can follow or not. You must choose whether or not to follow the directions provided by the Spirit."

"But how can I make that decision when I don't even know what the instructions mean."

"Your spirit knows what they mean and will reveal the meaning to you if you truly want to know. Not all people want to know the will of the Great Spirit. They will not ask the question of their own spirit because they do not want to be instructed. Many people do not fulfill their mission because they do not want to fulfill it. The opportunity is there but many choose to follow their own pursuits. The Spirit is patient. The Spirit does not demand, but the Spirit is ready at any time to assist the process for those who are truly ready to serve. Your dream has come to instruct your spirit. You can learn the meaning of those instructions if you want to know. The message came in symbols so you have a choice. You do not have to know. Star Man, Jesus, did much of his teaching in symbols for that reason when he was on earth. He spoke to men's hearts in symbols for those who truly wanted to know but did not force his message on anyone who was not ready. You can learn the meaning of your dream if you want to know. You can ask your spirit and it will reveal it to you when you are ready to hear. But do not ask unless you truly want to know."

He stood up and left the room without saying good-bye. I was somewhat surprised by the abruptness of his departure, but I had learned from previous encounters with Flying Eagle that when he was in his teaching mode the end of a lesson was the end.

18

The dream stayed on my mind for days. I thought about it, I meditated about it and I wrote in my journal about it, but nothing became clear to me. It was obvious that the cup could be a communion symbol and that the wound was reminiscent of the wound in Star Man's hand and of the crucifixion, but why the meadow, why three cycles into the cave; what did the dead tree represent? I could go no further. Finally I asked Flying Eagle for help with it in one of our sessions.

"I still don't understand my spirit dream," I said. "Some of the symbols seem obvious, others are confusing. It's not coming together for me."

"The reason you do not understand the dream is that you are not yet ready to hear the answer," he said. "You do not want to know the answer. If you did, you would have asked your spirit for the meaning of the dream. It knows the answer."

"But I thought I was asking my spirit for the answer. I have been thinking about it; I have been meditating about it and I have been journaling about it. I don't seem to get any answers beyond the obvious symbols of the cup and the wound."

"The dream does not mean what you think it means. You want it to tell you what to do. The dream is not telling you what to do; it is telling you how to be. You are still so caught in your world of doing that your are not yet ready to hear your dream's message about how to be."

"I'll think more about that," I said.

"That is the problem. You think about things. For you, thinking is another thing that you do. The dream is not about doing and the answer to it will not come from more doing. You must enter the realm of being. When you do, the meaning of the dream will come clear."

Again the session ended abruptly. I was left alone.

I started thinking about what Flying Eagle had said. Then I realized I was doing more of what he suggested that I not be doing; I was thinking. I tried not to think about what he said. Then I started thinking about not thinking about what he had said. Finally I admitted to myself with a smile that, just as Flying Eagle had said, I was still caught up in doing. I realized how much I relied on thinking and other forms of doing. My education and culture had trained me to solve problems through doing. Doing was the road to success. The more one was willing to do, the more one would achieve. But now I found myself in a situation where just the opposite was true; doing was not providing me with the meaning of the dream.

"How do I be?" I said to myself and smiled. The words of the question sounded like Old English. "I be fine when I be," I mused. Still trying to solve the problem by thinking, I thought about the times in my life when I had been most in touch with my being side. It occurred to me that while I was waiting in the forest for an animal, or waiting for evil, or waiting for Star Man to come, I had been in a state of being. The animals seem to know how to wait. Maybe it was time to go back to the forest and wait.

Every afternoon I went into the forest and waited. I wasn't even quite sure what I was waiting for; perhaps I was just waiting for the sake of waiting. As before, the waiting seemed like hard work at first but as I continued with it, the periods of silence became enjoyable and started taking on an importance of their own. A part of my inner self was being fed when I sat and did nothing for hours.

Then one afternoon about four P.M., as I was sitting in the forest, I heard a rustling sound in some branches above my head. I looked up and saw a large hawk sitting on a limb about twenty feet off the ground. We looked at each other for a few minutes, then he flew down to the ground and landed a few feet away in front of me. Again we looked at each other in silence. I waited. Perhaps thirty minutes later he spoke.

"You have come with questions about yourself," he said.

"Yes," I said out loud. "I want to know the meaning of a dream I had. I want to learn how to be. But first, I want to know about you. Why have you come to me? The last time I talked with a deer."

"I have come because you have questions about yourself. I am your power animal. I am here to teach you how to be more fully yourself. I must warn you that you will not like some of what I have to teach you. To ask about oneself is to ask for the good and the bad, the parts of yourself you consider acceptable, and the parts you have rejected and experience only in others."

"I want to hear it all, the good and the bad."

"All right. I will proceed." He paused as though he were thinking and then continued. "Some say a hawk is bad because it hunts and kills other animals for food, but that is neither good or bad; it is the way the Creator planned for hawks to survive. When I am being myself, when I am hunting, I am following the Creator's plan for me. The Creator's plan is beyond good and bad, the Creator's plan is simply the way things are, the way things were created to be. We call the Creator good, but that is our value that we have placed on the Creator. The Creator just is.

"I am going to tell you some things about yourself. Some of the things I say may seem bad to you, other things may seem good. None of the things are good or bad. Good or bad is a value you place on things. When you truly believe that, it will set you free to experience what is, the way it is, without any judgements.

"You have questions about your dream. You are not ready to understand the dream because it is about death. The way to live fully is to die. You are not ready to die so you can not understand that death is the answer to life. Your life lacks power. In order to live fully you must die."

"You sound like St. Paul. He said some things like that."

"I am not here to talk about St. Paul or about your religion. I am here to talk about you and about the life of power. Your knowledge of other teachers has done you little good because you did not take them seriously. When they taught you that death was the key to life you decided that they were speaking figuratively. You reinterpreted what they were saying. You removed the power from their teachings by agreeing with them on the figurative level. Do not do that to what I have to say to you. I am speaking of deep truths. Do not avoid their power by agreeing with them in principal. Your greatest block to growth is that you agree with too much. You need to fight with the truth to discover its power. Agreement is not the path to discovery; struggle is. Struggle with this truth, fight against the reality of death, resist it with all your might. You can not agree your way into relationship with the truth.

"You," he continued, "do not want to be a warrior. You do not want to struggle. But you must learn to struggle, to fight, to conquer; therein lies your power. And when you are ready to fight with the truth you are ready to be conquered by the truth. The truth must be resisted before it can conquer you."

"But if I agree with something, how can I fight against it?"

"That is exactly the point I am making. You agree too quickly. You agree in order to avoid the conflict. The Spirit comes in power to those who are ready to fight. Power does not come to those who like to sit around and agree with ideas. Most of your people have not learned that and neither have you. You want to learn without struggle.

"I am your power animal. I represent those things that you are unwilling to accept in yourself. I hunt. I kill. I am a symbol for warriors. You do not like what I represent. You are afraid of what I represent. You are afraid of death. Until you are ready to hunt, to kill or to be killed, you are not worthy of my time. I will not return until you are ready to do all three." The hawk slowly turned until his back was facing me, then dramatically lifted his tail feathers and defecated. He turned his head and looked at me as if to see if I had gotten his point and then leaped into the air and flew off through the trees.

19

The next time I saw Flying Eagle I told him about my encounter with the hawk, including the manner in which he had departed. Flying Eagle slapped me on the back and roared with laughter. He started to compose himself and then burst into laughter again.

"It's funny, but it's not that funny," I said without smiling.

"Oh Little Warrior," he said with tears streaming down his face, "you take yourself too seriously. That hawk is a better teacher than I am. He showed you what I have been unable to get across to you for weeks," he snickered. "You, as a man of peace, ain't worth shit," and he roared with laughter again. Finally Flying Eagle composed himself, looked at me seriously and said, "What do you think about the hawk's teachings?"

"Well, it wasn't what I wanted to hear...or see." I finally cracked a smile. "That stuff about death being the key to life is still confusing to me. I'm not quite sure what he meant, but I must say, I'm not too excited about the subject. Death is not something I look forward to."

"You don't have to look forward to it. Some actually do, but that is not necessary. What is important is the encounter. You resist the encounter with death. Until you are willing to have that encounter you will not be effective."

"So how do I have this encounter with death? Do I deliberately walk out in front of a Mack truck or something?"

He looked serious.

"Some do," he said, "but after the truck is finished with them they ain't worth shit as men of peace or as warriors." And he roared with laughter again.

I was getting a little tired of his humor, but I had to admit it was funny, and I laughed with him that time.

When he regained his composure he said, "It is not necessary for you to meet death in that way. You must meet its meaning. Some people do meet its meaning in a close encounter with physical death. Warriors often have that experience, but anyone can meet death's meaning by allowing the full realization to sink in that they are going to die. All of us are going to die someday. Most of us find ways to avoid the reality of that. We think someday is a long way away; we think it is something that happens to others but is not really going to happen to us; or we agree too quickly with the statement that we are going to die and in that way avoid the full experience of its reality. You must struggle with the reality of death. You must resist it and fight it and get in touch with your fear of it and become aware of your longing for a universe that does not have death. Most of all you must become aware of your anger at the Creator for making a universe in which you will have to encounter death. Only then can you experience the Creator's gift to you.

"Most people," he continued, "are afraid of their anger at the Creator. They believe in the deeper levels of themselves that the Spirit will kill them or blot them out of existence if they get angry enough. They do not truly believe that God is love and that love is strong enough to accept their underlying rage. We must test it. All of us must test it by getting in touch with the reality of our own impending death and our fury with God for not sparing us from death. Until we have done that we can not fully accept the gift that life does not end. The secret of the universe is that a loving Creator did in fact make a universe that does not have death in it, but each of us must discover that for ourselves and we must discover it through experience. Knowledge is not enough."

"Are you really saying that death does not exist?"

"Yes. The appearance of death exists. People who walk out in front of trucks get flattened and we bury them. We say they have died, but they continue to live. Life does not end when death comes to the physical body. But knowledge of that fact is not enough. You must confront your own death before you are able to live fully in the reality that it does not exist. Do you understand?"

"Yes, I do."

"But understanding is not enough and understanding will not make it real for you. You must experience it, Little Warrior. Then you will own that knowledge and can live out of that reality." He stopped talking and walked away.

❧ 20 ❧

I was being asked to face the certainty of my own death and thereby discover for myself the reality of a universe without death. Of course it didn't make sense, but no paradox makes sense; that is part of its power. In a paradox the truth is there but it is clearly in the silence between the words.

I thought about the times in my life when I had had brushes with death, the car accident that almost happened, engine trouble on an airplane flight and the fall out of my tree house as a youngster. Each of those was a brief but real encounter with the possibility of death. I tried to remember how I had responded to them at the time. Had I met the reality of death in the way that Flying Eagle said was necessary? Obviously I had not. What had I done to prevent the experience from being that all important full encounter with my own mortality? I remembered being scared in the midst of each of those experiences, but in each case I had soon turned that brush with death into further evidence of my own invincibility. Death had come near but it had not taken me. I had been aware that death could come to others but my experiences had not blotted out my denial that death would ever come for me.

So how could I face death's reality now? Flying Eagle obviously didn't think my Mack truck approach was necessary. What was it that death represented to me? What made death so frightening?

When I thought about the experience on the airplane with engine trouble I remembered an awful feeling of being totally out of control of my life. I hadn't thought about it much afterward; but I now realized that, at that point, my fear of being out of control had been greater than my fear of my life coming to an end.

I thought about how many people had said to me in all seriousness that they would rather die than live on totally paralyzed. The prospect of losing control of one's life or destiny seems to be more fearsome to many of us than the loss of life itself. Perhaps I too was more strenuously avoiding loss of control in the presence of death than I was avoiding death itself. Then the thought occurred to me that if I were so unwilling to give up control of my life, how could I ever yield to the will of the Spirit?

If I truly believed that the Spirit was love, would that make a difference? Would I then be able to give up my control and place it in the hands of Love itself? I wondered.

The next time I met with Flying Eagle I said, "I've been thinking a lot about death and what makes it so powerful for me. I believe I am really afraid of the loss of control that I associate with dying. But that brings me to the question of why I am so afraid of losing control?

"I have decided that it's because I don't really believe God is love. If I truly believed that God is love, it would feel safe to give up control to him.

"Am I on the right track?"

"You are close to the truth, Little Warrior. You are not there yet, but you are close."

"So what's missing?"

"You have not yet discovered what makes you vulnerable when you lose control. Knowing that God is love is important but not enough. Evil knows that God is love and it does not cause evil to serve God willingly. The part of you that creates evil already knows that God is love but you continue to create evil. There is more. You are on the right track but there is more."

I waited, but he said no more. It was clear that he was not going to provide me with the missing part of the answer; he still expected me to work it out myself.

≈ 21 ≈

My thoughts kept returning to the issue of why I am so threatened when I lose control. I searched for an answer for days. I even asked Flying Eagle for more help with it. He politely refused and told me that I would know the answer when I found it.

That didn't help. The struggle dragged on.

Then one day as I walked through the forest with nothing in particular on my mind, I had an insight. Into my mind flashed the words, "I am God in my own universe." I stopped dead in my tracks. The feeling that I was onto something hit like a bolt of lightning. I had heard those words years before in a workshop I had attended. The leader had been making the point that we create our own reality, but his statement hit me now with new and different implications. "I am God in my own universe." Could that be the answer? Had I made myself God by putting myself at the center of my own universe? I wondered. Outwardly I didn't act like a self-centered God. But maybe I was just well socialized? Perhaps I have practiced manners and socially acceptable behaviors in order to hide my self-centeredness from myself and from others. The more I thought honestly about it the more I realized that I really did want to be God, that my will was central and that I worshipped myself as the most important thing in my own universe. Meeting my own needs and finding fulfillment and happiness for myself was of utmost importance to me.

I did not like the vision of myself as self-centered and self-serving, but it was accurate and it explained a lot. Any loss of control would challenge my whole system; I could not be out of control and be God at the same time. Loss of control would mean loss of my deity. And I realized that I was even more afraid of losing my deity than I was of losing my life. I had found the answer.

Over the rest of the day I continued to think about the issue of being God in my own universe. I remembered that in my religion the serpent had told Adam and Eve that if they ate the fruit they would "be like God, knowing good and evil." Was that the ultimate temptation for all mankind, to be like God and to have his knowledge? Could original sin be that desire to be one's own God?

When I saw Flying Eagle I told him about my discovery.

"You have done well, Little Warrior," he said. "Now you are ready to make the choice."

"What choice?" I asked naively.

"The choice of whom you will serve. Are you going to serve yourself as God or to serve the Spirit as God."

The choice seemed obvious. I should serve the Spirit, but it had become clear to me that a very real part of me did not want the Spirit as my God.

"How can I choose to let the Spirit be God in my life when I really want to be God myself?" I asked.

"There is only one way," Flying Eagle said gently. "The only thing that is stronger than your desire to be God is your desire to experience love itself. When you realize that the Spirit truly is love, you will be free to choose to serve the Spirit as your God."

I thought about what he said. St. Paul had talked about all people being by nature in bondage, slaves to self. It was starting to make sense to me in a new way. And the way out of that bondage is to serve the God of love, "whose service is perfect freedom."

"So it all boils down to believing that God is love. If I don't believe God is love, I don't have any hope of breaking free of always, at the core, serving myself."

"You got it!" he said with a little smile. "But knowing it with your mind is not enough. You must know that God is love with your heart."

"How do I do that? How do I make it real?"

"Your spirit already knows the answer," he said. "Look to your spirit dream. It is telling you the answer."

He turned and walked away.

❧ 22 ❧

I took a walk into the forest and sat down on a moss covered rock to think. Flying Eagle had stressed the importance of experiencing God as love, and both the hawk and Flying Eagle had declared my need to encounter death. Were the two related in some way? Were both themes in my dream? I thought about Star Man's wound and the wound in my dream. The wound could clearly be a symbol of suffering and death; could it also be a symbol of love? I remembered Jesus' statement that, "Greater love has no man than this, that a man lay down his life for his friends." The wound did seem to represent both death and love.

St. Paul talked about being crucified with Christ. Did he mean that the self-centered part of him died on the cross with Jesus? Is it possible for the God of love to take my self-centered God with him now to die on the cross? Is that why I am both attracted to the wound and terrified of it. Am I both attracted to and terrified of love because it can cause a death of self in me? I think so. If love becomes the center of my life I can no longer be the self-centered God of my life. By accepting the cup was I accepting the death of self, even asking for it somehow? In the dream, when I drank from the cup I was ejected into a beautiful world; that could represent the beauty of the world when encountered with love at the center of my life. But after a time I had to return to the wound and repeat the cycle again; was the death of self as God a continual process of renewal, of having myself as God die with Christ and experiencing myself as love raised from the dead with Christ? It was a different way for me to think about it but it was starting to fit together.

But what about the end of the dream, with me sobbing at the foot of a dead tree? What did that mean? That part continued to confuse me.

I went to Flying Eagle and told him what I had been able to figure out about the symbols in the dream. He listened intently and then said, "You seem to be on the right track, but you have not mentioned the rituals. Does the dream speak to you about the rituals?"

"Yes, I think so. In the dream I am drawn into the wound and drink from the cup three times. I think it is telling me that I need to experience the ritual of communion repeatedly in order to keep replacing my self-centered side with love. Doing it once does not seem to be sufficient to solve the problem permanently."

"I think that you are right. For you it is important to receive communion. My spirit dream pointed to my need to do the Eagle Dance regularly in order to experience my freedom from self. Our traditions are different but the principal is the same. Do you understand the end of your dream yet?"

"No, I don't. Why am I in grief at the dead tree?"

"This much I will tell you," he said. "My dream too ended with my experiencing deep grief. Men's spirit dreams often have grief in them. It is because for a man the path of inner freedom requires coming face to face with deep inner grief. For women the path may be different. For women it involves pain also but the pain is not always grief. As a man, you must face and experience your deep inner grief in the presence of love. It is a grieving for self, a grieving for the death of your own deity, a grieving for life not having given you what you thought you needed. The wound is Star Man's but the wound is also your own. You are wounded like him and love will make you grieve. You too, my friend, must become 'a man of sorrows, and acquainted with grief' if you allow yourself to be transformed by love."

"But why is it that way? Why does love have to bring so much pain with it? I thought love was supposed to be wonderful and joyous and fulfilling."

"It is all that and more. But those feelings don't come in the early stages. You see, love is not what you thought it was. Love is not just the ability to feel good about another; it is the ability to suffer for another. If you want to be truly overwhelmed by love you must first be prepared to suffer and you must meet your own grief."

In his customary manner he turned abruptly and walked away.

❧ 23 ❧

I didn't like what Flying Eagle had taught me about love. I wanted a universe where love involved only warm and tender feelings, not one in which love could also bring pain and suffering. I was deeply disappointed, but more than that, I was angry. I walked deep into the forest, out of ear shot of the village. I kicked stones and fallen branches off the path in fury as I went. I cursed, under my breath at first, then out loud and finally at the top of my lungs. Everything seemed to be caving in on me. All my cherished illusions about life were slipping away and I didn't like what was left. I was angry at God for allowing the universe to be the way it was. I wanted love to be beautiful. It felt ugly. I didn't want to be in a universe where love could be defined as the ability to suffer for another person. I thought about the pain and suffering that I had experienced in some of the relationships that I had valued most in my life. My fury at being hurt by my parents and others returned but now it was fury not at them for being imperfect, but at God for allowing love to be so painful.

Star Man's wound was haunting me. It was ugly, even revolting, but I couldn't get it out of my mind. I shut my eyes and tried to block out the thoughts that were racing through my head. All I could visualize was that hideous, gaping wound and the thought that that is what love looks like. It was disgusting. It wasn't fair. In my universe love isn't like that. My universe...there it was again. I was God in my own universe. I had created a false reality, one where love was the way I thought it should be. In my universe love didn't look like that wound. It should always be beautiful, as I had created it, not the way the true God of the universe proclaimed it could be.

I continued to struggle for hours. I wanted my universe not God's. I wanted my kind of love, not his, to be real. I continued to rant and rave and curse and fume.

Finally I started to grieve. The pain engulfed me. I collapsed on the ground and sobbed. I was grieving the loss of my universe. I was grieving the loss of my illusions. I was grieving over the possibility that love would never seem beautiful again. The agony I experienced was almost unbearable.

Then slowly, very slowly, I began to accept love as it really was. Although, I didn't like reality as I was now seeing it, I was no longer able to create what I now knew to be an illusion. I was defeated, conquered by a vision of love that I detested. I stopped trying to be God.

Suddenly the process I had been experiencing reversed and everything started coming back together again. I realized that just as I had suffered tremendous pain in relationships with those I loved, that they too had suffered pain in their relationship with me. If love is truly the ability to suffer for another person then the suffering that we had all experienced was not a cruel anomaly, it was a healthy experience of the power of love. Suffering is, at times, a normal part of love and the willingness to endure suffering is an expression of love. The suffering I went through as a result of my parents' imperfections was an expression of my love for them. Their suffering from my imperfections was an expression of their love for me. I had always assumed that I had suffered because they had not loved me enough or not in the right ways. But now I saw that it was because we had loved each other that we had been able to experience such pain in our relationship.

Could one's expression of love for God be found in one's willingness to live in an imperfect world with imperfect people and willingly suffer the pain that such engagements inflicted? Could God's love for us be found in His willingness to suffer? Star Man's wound started to make sense in a way that it never had before. His wound was a picture of love.

Love started to seem beautiful again and, strangely enough, the image of the wound started to be beautiful as well. I started seeing love in places where I had been blind to it before. I had wanted a life that was free of pain; now I wanted to engage my pain and the pain of others in my life. Pain was beautiful, love was beautiful, life was beautiful.

I returned to the village still reeling from my discovery of beauty in the most unlikely of places. I found Flying Eagle and tried to explain to him what I had just experienced but everything I said seemed flat and empty in comparison to the experience of discovery I had just had.

"The wound is now beautiful," he said finally, summarizing many minutes of my seemingly incoherent sputtering.

"Yes," I said with a sigh.

"That is good," he said. He patted me on the shoulder and departed.

❧ 24 ❧

I thought a lot about what was happening to me. My understanding of the world was changing. My understanding of myself was changing. My understanding of good and evil was changing. And now my understanding of love was changing. I had come to Flying Eagle to learn about his religion but he had taught me about my own. The next time we met together I said, "I'm not complaining, but why have you been talking so much about my religion instead of yours when you teach me about the Spirit?"

"I have taught you about your own religion but I have also been teaching you about mine. Our religions talk about the Spirit in different ways but they are dealing with the same truth. The words are different but the truth is the same. I have been leading you to the truth that is found between the words. That is the true nature of religion. Many people think that religion is about the words or the forms of the rituals that are used. The words and the rituals are dependent upon the culture of the people who are seeking the Spirit. That has caused your people much misunderstanding. Your religion originated with a people far away who lived in tribes in an arid land and who fought for control of their territory. In this country most of your people live in a lush land whose borders are secure. The words used to point to truths about the Spirit came from a Hebrew culture that is quite foreign to your own. Even the Lord's Prayer, which people of your faith use so frequently, came through a people who understood the role of a father quite differently from the way it is understood in your culture today. The words of that prayer came through their culture. Your people seem to assume that those words convey the truth and that they do it equally as well in your culture as they did in the culture of Jesus' time. But the words don't convey the truth; they point to a truth between the words and they point with images that are now foreign to your people. Your religion has lost much of its relevance for your people because you are using words from a different culture and time. You must allow the Spirit to speak to your time and to your culture through images that point between the words to truths that your people can experience. Your people are lazy; they keep borrowing the words of another culture and expecting to find the whole truth in those words. Your job is to discover the truth in your culture, not in someone else's. I can tell you of my religion. I can tell you about the words that we use and about the rituals that we have evolved but they will not lead you to the truth unless you look between the words and discover the truth for yourself. Don't look for the Spirit in our culture. You will never come to understand the Spirit deeply in that way. You must allow the Spirit to speak to you in the silence between the words from your culture. Do you understand?"

"Yes, I think so. But isn't there some value for me in studying your religion. Can't I learn things about the Spirit in that way that I haven't learned in my religion?"

"Yes you can. The Spirit had some different things to reveal to the people of my culture than it did to the people of Israel. But what is truly important is not learning with your mind, it is learning with your heart, learning to listen for what the Spirit is saying to you rather than trying to discover what the Spirit is saying to us. I am here to teach you about my religion and what I know of the Spirit. Star Man told me to do that. But you must understand that learning about my religion is never a satisfactory substitute for directly hearing the voice of the Spirit yourself. If you understand that it will save you much trouble in life. Look for the voice of the Spirit where the Spirit speaks most clearly to you, through the silence between the words and images of your own culture.

"You still look puzzled. I can tell that this concept still seems foreign to you but it should not. Jesus taught what I have been telling you today. He did away with The Law not because The Law was wrong but because The Law had come forth at a time when the nomadic tribes were in the process of finding and settling in a new homeland. The image of finding the Spirit within the context of law and structure had far different meaning then than it did later when their culture was fully settled in the land. The people had come to believe that the truth was in The Law and in obeying The Law. It never was. The truth had always been in the silence between the words of The Law. When the people forgot that, The Law became a hindrance to hearing the Spirit rather than the aid that it had been in the early days. That is so with your religion now. Your people think that the words of your religion are sacred and that knowing and following their concepts is the same as knowing the Spirit. It is not

so and your religion has become, for many, a hindrance to their relationship with the Spirit."

"You seem to enjoy talking about Christianity," I said.

He smiled. "I can't resist teaching Christians about their own faith. So
many of them have talked down to us through the years and told us that
we do not know the truth. It is fun to show them what has been right
under their noses while they had their noses held so high in the air.
Humor me and let me speak. I have so little opportunity to expound
about Christianity with someone who will not be offended by what I
have to say."

"I love it," I said. "I am beginning to understand some things about
my religion for the first time. But how did you learn about all this?"

"I've done some reading," he said, "but mostly I've listened to Star
Man. It's amazing what you can learn about Christianity from talking to
Star Man." He smiled slyly and walked away.

❧ 25 ❧

The sun was bright. It was a hot day. It seemed as if I had been climbing for hours. Actually, I had been on the trail for less than an hour, but its steepness made each yard an agony. I was puffing heavily. Flying Eagle had told me to meet him on top of the mountain at noon. Another thirty minutes and I would be there, if I lasted that long. I sat down to rest again. I took a sip of water from my canteen and surveyed my surroundings. It was then that I saw the five foot rattle snake less than a yard from the rock where I was sitting. At first I reacted in horror. My heart sank and I involuntarily jumped to my feet. But instead of dashing to a safe distance something caused me to hesitate. There was something peculiar about the snake. It was not coiled for an attack despite the fact that it had obviously seen me, and my sudden movements would normally have resulted in some sort of reaction. There was something peaceful in its posture. I stood still and looked at the snake. It appeared to be watching me.

Cautiously, I sat down again, kept looking at the snake and waited. Finally it spoke.

"You have come a long way," it said. "You have come to understand things that you did not know before but you are in danger of using your knowledge as a substitute for an experience of the truth. Do not do that. Do not allow yourself to think of the truth as something to be learned instead of something to be experienced. There is great danger in that. You have come to know about good and evil, but you must also experience good and evil on a deeper level or you will not know the truth. The evil that you experience in the world comes from within you. You have learned that concept but unless you experience the reality of it more fully you will not be changed by it. Experience changes people. Knowledge does not. Knowledge is merely a way to understand, to make sense of, what is experienced. If you stop short of experiencing the full power of evil within you you will have gained nothing."

"But what about my experience by the fire when I met my evil side and remembered the massacre? Doesn't that count for anything?" I protested.

"Yes. But that was an experience of the reality of your evil. It was not, for you, a full recognition of its power. Evil is still your enemy rather than your friend. Evil can be your friend, but you first must accept it more deeply as a part of yourself. Some draw power from the evil within them. Some draw power only from the good. But the true warrior draws power from the union of good and evil."

"How do I do that?"

"By being open to the truth. Until now you have been struggling to see yourself as good out of the illusion that your goodness comes from the good that you do. Even after you remembered your involvement in the massacre and accepted the reality of your evil nature, you continued to try to convince yourself that you were basically good because you are now doing more good than evil.

"A man whose heart is good is not a man who does only good things; he is a man who is capable of embracing all that is true about himself. You have that ability but you have not yet fully exercised it. You are teachable because you have the potential to see both good and evil within yourself. The time has come for you to do that. The pathway to the spirit is found in both your good and your evil nature. It is where the two come together that you will find the true power of the warrior." Having said that, the snake crawled off and disappeared under a large rock.

❧ 26 ☙

When I finally reached the top of the mountain I found Flying Eagle waiting for me. He looked refreshed. I was exhausted.

"You're late," he said. "I've been waiting for you."

"How did you get here?" I asked, still breathing hard.

"Little Warrior, you always do things the hard way. They don't call me Flying Eagle for nothing."

I chuckled. He did not.

I had a strange sensation. Suddenly I could not tell whether he was joking or serious.

When he had told me that morning to meet him on top of the mountain we were in the village. I had left him there and immediately started up the trail. Other than short stops to rest and to talk to the snake, I had climbed constantly. Flying Eagle had not passed me on the trail. I was puzzled. How could an 83-year-old man, making his own trail, climb faster than I had and look perfectly rested? I was less than half his age and was nearly exhausted. I was about to ask him about it again when he changed the subject.

"Did you meet anyone on the trail?" he asked casually.

I told him about my encounter with the rattle snake and the substance of our conversation.

"The last time I took that trail I met that snake," he said. "He speaks wisdom. I wondered if you would meet him today? He is an expert on evil."

"How did you get up here?" I asked, returning to my question.

"We'll talk about that later," he said. "Did you understand what the snake taught you?"

"No, I'm still confused."

"Little Warrior, if you look deeply into yourself you will find both good and evil. You cannot have one without the other. They are two sides of the same mirror. Both those who deny the reality of evil within and those who resist it limit their own power. Jesus said not to resist evil but you did not take his saying seriously. You must face the evil within and embrace it. In so doing you will discover that evil does not exist. But in order to discover that evil does not exist you must first discover that it does exist."

"That makes perfect sense," I said rolling my eyes in a big semicircle.

"It does not make sense to you now, but it will. The problem with you Christians is that you keep forgetting your own theology. You proclaim that you believe in one God and then go merrily along acting as though there were a God of good and another God of evil. Don't you get it? They are the same. The power is in the unity not in the separation. Christians seem to keep trying to gain power by separating themselves from evil. The two are the same. That acknowledgement is what gives the true warrior his power. You lack power because you are still trying to be good. You will gain power when you try merely to be whole. The warrior becomes whole when he engages his enemy. You will become whole when you fully embrace your evil nature and when you do that, you will discover that what is evil is good."

I sensed that he was about to leave me. "Why did you ask me to come up here?" I asked.

"For two reasons," he said. "Because I thought it was time for you to meet the snake and because I wanted you to ask me how I got up here. You have a lot to think about. I'll see you back in the village."

He headed off over the rocks and disappeared from view. Five minutes later I noticed an eagle circling over head. Three times it descended and swooped only a few feet above my head. On the third pass it flew off in the direction of the village. I sat in amazement.

"You have a lot to think about," I muttered, echoing Flying Eagles words. "They don't call me Flying Eagle for nothing."

﹋ 27 ﹌

I sat on the mountain top thinking, meditating and taking in the view for several hours. It was pleasant but no new insights or revelations came to me. Finally the combination of the heat and a nearly empty canteen caused me to start my return to the village. Although the descent went much faster, in some ways it was more difficult than the climb. It was a struggle to fight gravity and maintain control as I came down the steep trail. As I clambered over the rocks I thought about the old saying, "It's not the fall that kills you; it's the sudden stop at the bottom." I wondered if that same general principle could be present in my struggle to get in touch with my own evil. Clearly some people had been taken over by their own evil and lost control, committing murder or other crimes as a result. An uncontrolled fall could make the bottom of the mountain a place of destruction, but with a controlled descent, as I was doing now, the bottom of the mountain could be a friendly environment. When the rattle snake told me that I must get in touch with my own evil, I had envisioned the process as being more like an uncontrolled fall than a gradual, intentional descent. Could the descent into one's own evil be a positive experience if done gradually, taking care not to lose control of the process?

I stopped to rest at the spot where I had encountered the rattle snake. There was no sign of him this time. I thought about my initial reaction to the snake. At first I had made the snake into an evil threat and had reacted instinctively to protect myself. But by remaining in control, by not resisting the evil, I had made room to experience the same snake as good and to learn from the encounter. Could that be what Jesus had in mind when he said, "Do not resist one who is evil"? Is it possible that the reality of evil does indeed exist only within us rather than in the object that we perceive as evil and that by not resisting evil we clear the way to discover that evil does not really exist apart from us?

When I reached the village Flying Eagle was waiting for me. As I walked over to him he held up his hand and said, "No questions about the eagle. We will talk about that later. First, we must talk about evil."

I told him about the insights I had while coming down the trail. He nodded thoughtfully as I spoke.

"Your illustration of how the snake changed from evil into good needs a little work but basically your understanding is correct, Little Warrior."

"Well if it is basically correct then how does the role of the warrior fit into all this? If evil really does not exist why is it the warrior's job to resist it?"

"You misunderstand the role of the warrior, my friend. The primary function of the warrior is to establish boundaries. The warrior does not fight against evil; the warrior stands firm at the boundaries. In establishing the boundaries, the evil that is within is projected outward and one experiences it in one's enemy. It is only when the boundary is threatened that the true warrior is called upon to fight. Some warriors never fight. But the fight is not truly against evil; the fight is against the violation of the boundaries."

"I don't understand," I said flatly.

"Look, you think that the fight is against evil. For the true warrior the fight is not against evil. Evil comes from within. It is when the warrior resists the evil itself that the warrior ceases to be a warrior and becomes a victim of the evil.

"The warrior's job is to establish distinctions. He declares that this thing and that thing are not the same. He establishes and defends the boundary between the two different things. He keeps things separate, distinct."

"But why is that important? What difference does it make?"

"All the difference. It is the boundaries that shape your life. It is the boundaries that give shape and meaning to who you are. It is when you encounter the boundaries that you know who you are and who you are not. You are not everything. In order to be something, rather than everything, there must be boundaries and they must be defended. The warrior defends the boundaries."

"O.K., but why not just say here is the boundary; on this side is me and on that side is not me and leave it at that."

"Because only in encountering the boundary do you discover who you are. You think that defining the boundary is enough. It is not. One must struggle with the boundary. One must defend the boundary. It is the boundary that prevents everything from becoming nothing."

"But I still don't understand why the boundary has to be defended. Why is the struggle important? Why isn't it enough merely to define the boundary and to know what is on each side of the boundary?"

"Because it is the struggle that makes the distinctions real for you. The universe is constantly changing while in totality it remains the same. It is the shifting of the boundaries that brings about change. You define who you are and how things will be by where the boundaries are. That is how you create, by drawing boundaries. Creation comes out of nothing. The totality of all that is is always nothing. Creation occurs by defining a boundary, making this different from that. As long as the boundary exists, that which was created exists. If the boundary moves, that which was created changes. It is the boundaries that determine what form creation takes. You create evil by drawing a boundary. You destroy evil by removing the boundary between good and evil. If the boundary does not exist then good and evil do not exist, they become nothing again. The warrior defends the boundaries. Without stable boundaries chaos exists as the creation heads toward nothingness again. Where chaos exists there is no growth.

"What you can experience as God is that which is within the boundaries that you yourself have established for goodness. The irony is that the same boundaries that allow you to experience God also limit your experience of God. In fact God is everywhere and in everything and can be encountered in all that is. As the scope of your own boundaries broaden, your experience of God will broaden. If you continue to grow, you will ultimately experience God in all that is and evil will cease to exist. Does that make sense?"

"Yes."

"There is one more important piece. God is love. The overriding principle of the universe is that the universe is always love, when taken in its totality. The boundaries may move, evil may thereby be created and encountered, but when the total picture is put together it is always love and God has always acted in love. Is that clear?"

"But that means that when you take in the whole picture evil is also an expression of love."

"You got it!" he almost shouted. I had never seen him so excited. "You got it," he said again. "You would be amazed at how many people can't get it even when it is laid out in front of them like that."

I was feeling uncomfortable. I had come to a rather obvious conclusion intellectually from what he had been saying but I was a long way from accepting that picture of evil as also being love.

"But I don't think I believe that," I said honestly.

"You don't now, but you will. You understood; that is what is important at this point. You do not know how unusual that is. Most people just can't get it. It won't compute in their brains. It is too strange for them to grasp. You grasped it because your heart is good. You have the capacity to incorporate the whole picture. That is what goodness truly is. Many people spend their lives running away from evil or denying its reality. They are unable to deal with it within themselves. People whose hearts are good are not good because there is no evil within them; they are good because they have the capacity to see good and evil in their broader context. Ultimately evil is good because it too is an expression of love. You create evil by drawing boundaries; but, when you grasp the total picture, evil disappears because all things are good when seen as a whole. Your Bible even tells you that. It says, 'in everything God works for good with those who love him.' Your job is not to resist evil but to incorporate it, to put it into the context of the whole, where it becomes good."

"But if I'm not supposed to resist evil why the Hell are you so determined that I need to become a warrior?"

"Because you must be able to defend the boundaries before you can understand their importance. In defending the boundaries you allow the distinction between good and evil to exist. In allowing the distinction to exist, you allow the possibility for the total picture to emerge and for evil to become good.

"Star Man told me that there is a process by which the creation is being recreated. First, the distinction between good and evil is established. Then evil is put in the larger context and becomes good. Recreation is the result.

"That is also the principle behind the resurrection. Jesus taught that resurrection is a normal process, but many in your religion misunderstand and think, despite what Paul said about it, that resurrection is something exclusive to Jesus. They even try to use Jesus' resurrection to prove his divinity. But there is no proof of his divinity. That is a matter of faith. He was merely the first to follow a natural process. He took death from its evil context as the end of life into its larger context of being the doorway into new life. Death became good. Recreation occurred. New life came forth out of death. Do you understand?

"Yes, I think so," I said. "And the function of the warrior is to defend the boundaries so that the distinction between good and evil can emerge as the first step toward recreation."

"That's right, Little Warrior. And there is a new warrior in you waiting to emerge. Do you understand that the time is drawing near when Little Warrior must face death in order to be recreated?"

"Yes, I do," I said solemnly.

"That is good. The old self must die for the self to be recreated. The time is near, you must be ready."

≈ 28 ≋

The thought of facing death was not appealing to me, whether it was physical death or merely the death of my old identity. I knew the truth even before he spoke but hearing him say it made it all seem more real. Death is a part of life. I knew that and I knew that at times old things have to die to make way for the new. But the thought of encountering the death of part of myself was something I dreaded. I have always had a strong urge to hang onto the familiar. I had established my own boundaries and grown so attached to their familiar locations that I had started treating them as though they were immovable. What if the boundaries were not immovable? What if I could change the location of the boundaries and thereby change the characteristics and limitations that define me as a person? Is that what Flying Eagle was urging me to do? He had told me that Little Warrior must die for the new warrior to emerge. If I changed the boundaries, Little Warrior and his set of characteristics would no longer exist and a new warrior would take his place. That was like Little Warrior dying. To change the boundaries would be to face the death of the old self. I wanted to discuss that with Flying Eagle. I sought him out and asked to speak with him.

"Tonight," he said. "We will talk tonight."

ꙮ 29 ꙮ

At around 8:00 P.M. I went to Flying Eagle's lodge. He was waiting for me. He invited me in and motioned me to one of two chairs facing each other next to a small table in the simply decorated room.

"Usually we talk in the forest," he said. "Tonight we will talk here."

I sat down facing him and reviewed for him my thoughts of that afternoon about changing one's boundaries and thereby experiencing the death of the old self.

"Your understanding is correct," he said. "In your religion it is called conversion. Conversion takes place when a person allows the boundaries to be moved. The old self dies and a new self emerges. The problem is that many of your people do not understand that this is a repeated process that can and should be experienced many times over the course of one's life. It is not an experience to have just once. The boundaries must be moved many times if one is to grow in understanding. It is by moving the boundaries that one is recreated and experiences new life. But each time the boundaries of the self are moved there is an experience of death of the old self. Most people fear death and are unwilling to allow the boundaries to move because they fear the death of the old self. They do not truly believe in resurrection, that new life comes forth out of death. Jesus taught that and he even demonstrated it when he was raised from the dead. But most of your people do not truly believe that death is the beginning of new life. Some believe it with their minds but few truly believe it with their hearts. In its narrow context death is the end of life and is evil. In its broader context even death is good because it is the means to bring about new life. As Star Man told me, the universe is constantly being recreated. Death is always the beginning of recreation. You understand that now. Are your ready to die, Little Warrior?"

"I still don't like it, but I think so."

"You don't have to like it. Death is not appealing to most of us, but it is necessary. It is time for you to die."

"How do I do it?"

"You already know how. You just don't know that you know. Death can come anywhere at any time. We could have had a ritual by the fire in the clearing but then you might have thought that you had to build a fire in order to die. I invited you here tonight so you would know that you can die anywhere. Good-bye, Little Warrior. I will not see you again as Little Warrior. It is time for you to die."

He stood up, then leaned over and kissed me gently on the cheek and left the room.

≈ 30 ≈

I sat in my chair in Flying Eagle's lodge for perhaps an hour. I thought about my life, about my joys and about my fears and about death. I felt sad. There was a part of me that did not want to say good-bye to myself as Little Warrior. I was grieving his impending death. Tears welled up and dropped gently into my lap. Finally, though still grieving, I felt ready to let go of my old identity. It was then that two memories came to my mind. One was from a course I took where the leader explained that metanoia, the Greek word translated as conversion in the Bible, was the term used when a person came to an intersection of his path and headed off in a new direction. The other memory was of the passage in the Wizard of Oz where the wizard transformed the Cowardly Lion into a creature of bravery by giving him a medal that said "courage". As I turned those two images of transformation over and over in my mind they came together as two complimentary parts of a whole. The first part was the decision to change one's direction and the second part was to make a corresponding change of the boundaries that define one's identity. When the lion accepted his medal, his boundaries shifted to include courage as part of his new identity. I thought about the practice of early Christians changing their names at their baptism or after some other experience that changed the direction of their lives. Could it be that simple? Could I recreate myself merely by deciding that I wanted to move in a new direction and then make a corresponding shift in the location of my self-defining boundaries? I decided to find out. I made a commitment to live my life out of a new identity as a man truly committed to the role of the warrior. Then I said good-bye to Little Warrior, rose from my chair and went outside.

☙ 31 ☙

Flying Eagle was waiting for me outside on the front steps of his lodge. As I emerged he stood up.

"Peace," he said.

"Peace," I responded.

"How do you feel?"

"Not much different," I admitted, "but I think I am different."

"You are different," he said with certainty. "You even look different. Little Warrior had a special way he always carried himself, kind of slouched at the shoulders. The slouch is gone and the light around you has changed. You are not the same, but it is good that you do not feel very different. Some do. Others don't. I have noticed through the years that those who feel different at first, have more difficulty adjusting to their new life after the feelings subside than those who do not feel so much at first. The change is not about feeling different; it is about being different."

"That's good to know. But I have this strange problem of not quite knowing who I am any more. I know I'm not Little Warrior now, but who am I?"

"Funny you should ask," he said, looking at me with a little grin spreading across his face. "A little bird told me, actually a rather big bird told me, that Screaming Hawk would be a good name for you. He came to me last night and said that you were about ready to become a serious warrior. By the way, he left me in a more dignified manner than he left you last time. You might find a conversation with him to be more fruitful now after the experience that you have had tonight. That hawk is really rather fond of you, you know."

"Thanks for telling me. Somehow his fondness for me slipped my notice."

"The warrior learns that sometimes it is necessary to be rough with people one cares about. Not all lessons are learned through gentleness and patience. At times one must be rude or crude to get a message across. Military leaders know that and for that reason they shout, insult and swear at their men when they are in training. People can not learn discipline without some rough treatment at times. The best leaders truly love those under them but they also know how to be rough when it is needed. The Spirit is that way too. As you may have noticed, the Spirit is not always nice. Some people think that a God of love should be nice all the time. They are confused by the Spirit allowing illness, calamity and suffering to exist. But a loving God would not be truly loving if all opportunities to learn discipline were removed. At times the Spirit uses evil to teach discipline. Evil is good too, remember? Don't resist evil. Resisting it only brings frustration and increases its power. Allow evil to exist. The Spirit uses it in many ways. Your job as a warrior is not to destroy evil but to contain it. Defend the boundaries. You can make evil good by putting it into its larger context, but don't ever confuse that mission with the idea of being called to destroy evil. For now, you need evil to exist and so does the Spirit. Remember that as you contend with evil. Warriors who forget that ain't worth shit.

"Little Warrior was more interested in being a man of peace than a warrior. There is nothing wrong with being a man of peace, but you must understand that being a man of peace is not better than being a warrior. Both are good. Little Warrior wanted to be a man of peace because he thought that was better, more right, more good than being a warrior. He did not understand. He was called to become a warrior but he resisted it because he thought being a man of peace was better. What is best is being what you are called to be. Whatever that is is good. Now you have a new name. Now you are Screaming Hawk. Screaming Hawk is a warrior. That is good. For Screaming Hawk to try to be something else would not be good. Be who you are within your own boundaries. When you are ready to be something else then you must change the boundaries and truly become something else. Is that clear?"

"Yes, but that still leaves me with the question of who I am. I'm Screaming Hawk. That's fine. I'm a warrior. O.K. But beyond that I don't know who I am. Do you understand what I'm saying?"

"You have become a new person and except in the broadest terms you don't know who you are now. So what did you expect? That when you became new that everything about you would be instantly clear and meaningful? My friend, your boundaries have changed. Your task, like everyone else's task in life, is to live out who you are, to discover what is within your boundaries and to express it. When you have accomplished that, your job is then to be recreated again and to explore within your new boundaries. That's what growth is all about. Of course you don't know who you are right now; that's for the Spirit to know and for you to find out."

"This is starting to make sense to me now. I am supposed to find out who Screaming Hawk is and be that."

"That's right; and when you have done that, you can, when you choose, be recreated into something else with different boundaries."

"Can I ever be a man of peace?"

"Yes, of course, but now you are Screaming Hawk and that is who you need to be now.

"But there is one more thing that you need to understand, Screaming Hawk."

"What's that?"

"You need to understand that you are Screaming Hawk now but that Screaming Hawk is not all that you are. You experience yourself as real within Screaming Hawk's boundaries but who you are goes beyond those boundaries. When the boundaries change, you experience what is within the new boundaries as being who you are. You can not experience the parts of yourself that are beyond the new boundaries even though they exist. Who you truly are is both the parts that you can experience and the parts of you that you can not now experience. Many people think that who they are is fixed and that they can only be what is presently within their boundaries. That is not so. You are free to experience different areas of life by changing the boundaries but, in a larger sense, you are always yourself even when your boundaries have changed what you can experience as you."

"So for now I am Screaming Hawk and for now I experience myself only by being Screaming Hawk. The parts of me that are beyond Scream- ing Hawk's boundaries can only legitimately be experienced when I change the boundaries and become some other form of myself."

"That's right. For now be Screaming Hawk with all your might."

"O.K. I will."

⚜ 32 ⚜

As the days passed, my new identity as Screaming Hawk felt quite comfortable in some areas but awkward in others. Some changes came immediately and effortlessly while others emerged slowly with much difficulty or not at all. It occurred to me that my transition was like that of a basketball player who is suddenly thrust into a football game for the first time. Some of the skills used in basketball, like running, are readily transferred to the new game but others, such as dribbling the ball, are useless, even counterproductive. As Screaming Hawk, I found a new sense of confidence when I expressed my feelings verbally but I continued to have great difficulty being aggressive even in situations where it was clearly needed. Flying Eagle confronted me about that one afternoon in the midst of one of our customary walks in the forest.

"A warrior cannot be a nice guy all the time, Screaming Hawk. When are you going to get that through your thick skull? Did you think that when you became a warrior that people were going to stand around and admire your ability to be polite in the midst of conflict? You are not at a cocktail party. Your social skills stand in your way as a warrior. Being a nice guy is not enough in life. At times you must be aggressive. People like politicians who are nice guys but they won't vote for them because they know on some level that they need someone who can really fight for what is important when the going gets rough. You are still trying to charm people into doing what is necessary. Part of your problem is that you grew up in a culture that does not understand the warrior very well. Your religious training was lacking in instruction about the role of the warrior. I bet somebody taught you in Sunday school that you are supposed to be nice to everybody, didn't they? That's bull shit! At times, Christians are called to be warriors. Jesus was a warrior.

"Jesus threw the money changers out of the temple. He was aggressive. I have never heard a Christian say that Jesus was aggressive. They talk about Jesus having had righteous indignation, as though that were an appropriate emotion, on rare occasions, even for a nice guy. They miss the point. He was aggressive. He went after the money changers. He was a warrior who was not afraid to act like one.

"Most of the Christians I know have placed narrow boundaries around Jesus. To them, Jesus was a nice guy who was a man of peace. But Jesus didn't have narrow boundaries; he had exceptionally wide boundaries. He was a man of peace but he was also a warrior. They didn't teach you that, did they? You Christians took the guts out of your religion when you tried to make Jesus into the all time nice guy. You will never fully understand Jesus until you realize that he was a warrior too. He even said that he came 'not to bring peace but a sword' and I bet your Sunday school teachers skipped right over that or said, 'Forget that children. He was just kidding. Remember Jesus was a nice guy and he wants you to be nice like him.' No wonder your religion lacks power! And you, my friend, are no different. You have created a nice guy God and a nice guy Jesus and you are trying to be a nice guy warrior. It's enough to make a good Indian want to puke! Get with it Screaming Hawk, the God you worship is too small! And as long as your God is too small, you also will be too small."

I thought about what Flying Eagle said. "You are right," I admitted. "I never thought of Jesus as a warrior and that view of him is very different from the picture of Jesus that I got growing up.

"But you said that Jesus had wide boundaries. Can you say more about that?"

"Yes. Jesus encompassed the breadth of his humanity. He was comfortable being the man of peace when needed or being the warrior when needed. You can find examples of both in the stories about him. With the crowd about to stone the woman caught in adultery he was a man of peace. With the money changers in the temple he was a warrior aggressively defending the boundaries. But most of all, Jesus was himself. Be very careful about trying to be like Jesus. You may end up drawing tight boundaries around some limited role that Jesus performed in some limited situation. You limit yourself by thinking that living within narrow boundaries is what being a Christian is all about.

Being a Christian is not about that. It is about discovering the Spirit in the midst of community. Don't you understand that? All those rules of conduct that you spend so much time teaching your kids in Sunday school is just that, rules of conduct, not Christianity. Christianity is about encountering the Spirit in the space between two or more people. That's what Jesus spent most of his time talking about. Look for it and you will see. In my religion the focus is on the encounter with the Spirit in the space between man and nature. Both religions are true. The Spirit is found in both places. I am not a Christian because my major focus is on encountering the Spirit in nature; my present boundaries encompass that realm of reality. You, my friend, are people oriented and you find the Spirit more easily, whether you know it or not, in the midst of encounters with other people. Do not try to be an Indian. Learn from us. Discover that the Spirit can be encountered in nature also, but do not abandon your natural orientation toward people. You will find the Spirit most powerfully among people because your boundaries now allow that.

"I am going to tell you something now that most of your people have not understood. I was troubled some years ago when Star Man first showed me his wounds. When I realized that Star Man was also Jesus I wondered if that meant that I should become a Christian. I had a conversation with Star Man about that. He told me something that was very interesting. He said that when, as Jesus, he had commanded the people to go forth into all nations and proclaim the Gospel, he was saying that for the good of the proclaimers as well as for the good of the people receiving what they proclaimed. You see, your Christian faith in not complete in itself. It is made more complete as it is spread to other peoples. You must learn about the Spirit from others. From the Indian you can learn about the Spirit as encountered in nature. From other peoples you can learn about other aspects of the Spirit. They in turn can learn about encountering the Spirit in community from those of you who truly understand Christianity. Your religion is made more complete as you encounter the truths of other peoples. But somewhere along the line you Christians misunderstood your commission and, for reasons that I do not understand, thought that Jesus was calling you to set up an exclusive religion as though it already encompassed all of the truth. Your missionaries started spreading Christianity, but instead of learning from the people they taught, the missionaries started telling the people that their old religions were all wrong, that Christianity had all of the truth.

"Star Man told me not to become a Christian. He said that one day a Christian would come to me prepared to learn the truth. You have come. You are open to learning about my religion. I am here to teach you about my religion but as you have already discovered I am also here to teach you about yours. If your missionaries had been as open to learning as they were to teaching, your religion would be more complete today."

"That certainly gives missionary work a different perspective," I said. "I had never thought of it in that way before."

✲ 33 ✲

I felt a new sense of dedication to the process of becoming a warrior. My old qualms about being a warrior had disappeared and the concept of being a Christian warrior no longer seemed like a contradiction of terms. I listened to Flying Eagle's teachings with a new sense of dedication and I started to really like the aggressive sound of my new name, Screaming Hawk. We talked in depth about my lifelong avoidance of my natural warrior traits and my fear of conflict.

"The problem is not aggression," Flying Eagle said one day as we walked, "but how one uses one's aggression. Aggression is power. Aggression is what leads one into battles with boldness. But battles are not bad in themselves. Some battles need to be fought. Others do not. Aggression that leads to fighting unnecessary battles is destructive. Aggression that leads to engaging in necessary conflicts is good. Some people have interpreted Jesus' teaching that we should love our enemies to mean that all conflict is wrong and that we should not have any enemies. That is not what Jesus meant. Love your enemies does not mean that you do not have any enemies, or that there is no need for the warrior. Quite the contrary. The true warrior is able to love those with whom he is in conflict because he knows that his enemies are those who carry the projections of his own inner evil. Our enemies are not necessarily evil; in many cases our enemies are those who merely have different values than our own. As you may have noticed, it is not unusual for peoples who have been at war with each other to be friendly allies just a few years later. Quite often it is unresolved issues rather than evil actions that cause conflict to erupt and one people to become the enemy of another people. In a war the warriors defend the boundaries, not just the physical boundaries of countries but also the boundaries that define the values of a people. It is the presence of poorly defined boundaries that causes more wars than anything else."

"But you seem so matter of fact about all this, Flying Eagle. In wars people get hurt and people get killed. Is that really necessary?"

"Yes. Not all wars can be avoided. For now some wars are necessary. But there is a time coming when men will learn how to draw and defend boundaries without physical conflict. Jesus made reference to that. You should strive for that time but also know that, for now, some wars must be fought and that some warriors must engage in physical combat."

"But I still don't understand why wars are necessary. Why must we do physical harm in order to resolve some issues?"

"When things are incomplete, issues are resolved through conflict. There is a time that is coming when your religion will be complete. Christians will have found and absorbed all of the important truths that are found in the religions of the world. When that occurs it will be possible for you to resolve conflict through peaceful means. Until that time physical violence will continue to be a necessary method to resolve some conflicts."

"Are you really telling me that we have wars because our religions are incomplete?"

"Yes, I am. Although your religion is still incomplete, it already contains all of the truths that are necessary for the beginning of the journey toward wholeness. But more is needed. Your people must obey Jesus' command to take your religion into all the world. When that command is obeyed and the truths in Christianity are truly merged with the basic truths in the other religions of the world, it will bring wholeness not only to individuals but to your religion as well. Wars and physical conflict come because of a lack of wholeness. Do you understand what I am saying? To put it another way, when the boundaries are too narrow the whole context can not be experienced and evil can not thereby be turned into good. By spreading your religion and incorporating other truths you enable yourself to have wider boundaries. When you have wider boundaries you are able to see the larger context and you can turn evil into good."

"But if the boundaries need to be wider why are warriors needed to defend the present position of the boundaries?"

"Because boundaries that are left unattended will shrink rather than expand. It is part of human nature to resist growth and to slide back into earlier levels of understanding. In defending the boundaries the warrior keeps the boundaries in their present locations. Without the warrior the boundaries contract, more and more is experienced as evil, and human growth is reversed."

"But don't the warriors also prevent growth by maintaining the position of the boundaries?"

"No. Growth is never gradual even though it may appear to be. New insights, new understandings, break into awareness suddenly and conflict follows. Then the new boundaries must be established and defended by the warriors. The warrior does not prevent the expansion of the boundaries. He prevents them from shrinking. Thus the warrior helps to maintain the growth that has occurred without preventing new growth."

"What you are telling me makes sense but it is very different from what I was brought up to think about these subjects. If all this is true, why wasn't I taught this by someone before now?"

"What I am teaching you is different but it is also the same. Most of what you were taught was not wrong, just incomplete. I am helping to fill in some of the gaps. As the gaps are filled, old information takes on new meanings for you. Remember the truth is not in the words; the truth is in the silence between the words. Look there for the truth of my teachings. There you will find the truth."

He changed the subject abruptly and commented on the beauty of the forest. We finished the walk in silence.

≈ 34 ≋

The sun came up like a large coal, glowing red in the sky. I had been up for hours meditating and thinking about what Flying Eagle had been teaching me. Although most of what Flying Eagle had said made sense, it was such a different way of looking at Christianity that my own religion no longer felt familiar to me. Christianity, rather than having an exclusive handle on the truth, has a built in flaw, a built in need to find its completion in other faiths. Could that mean that when Christianity is not encountering other religions and cultures it is stagnant. Is that part of the reason that Christianity seems devoid of meaning to so many people today? Are we needing new insights about the Spirit from other peoples in order to keep our own faith alive? Maybe so. Flying Eagle certainly thought so. Had I not come to Flying Eagle to learn about his religion because on some level I was experiencing an emptiness in my own? I came to find out what he believed but I discovered new depths of meaning in my own religion as a result. I needed a non-Christian to teach me about Christianity. But hadn't it always been that way? Had not some of the greatest theological insights come about through the collision of Christianity, with the concepts of the Greek and Roman world? Christianity had been broadened and changed by that contact. Are we lacking in that kind of contact today? Could the interest in Native American culture and religion, that I myself experienced, be born of an attempt to find completion for my own incomplete religion? And are not many of our present problems with the ecology a result of our failure to learn the respect for the earth that is so much a part of Native American religions? Our cultures had collided; the opportunity to learn had been there but we had failed to learn. How many battles had there been over the failure to understand the difference between the White's concept of individual ownership of the land as opposed to the Indians' concept that we merely own hunting rights on the Spirit's land? It seems that we are learning through hard lessons now that the land truly belongs not to us but to the Spirit.

I also thought about Flying Eagle's statement that Christianity is basically focused on encountering the Spirit in community. As I now looked at Christianity it seemed obvious that he was right. How had we ever gotten the idea that Christianity is primarily focused on our private relationship with God? Nearly everywhere I looked in the New Testament I found community. Nearly every place that the word "you" appears in the words of Jesus or St. Paul it is plural in the original Greek. Somehow I had always assumed that it was singular, that he had been speaking to the individual. Was the Christian message truly to the community of believers rather than to the individual? It seems so.

The Christianity that I grew up with was vastly different from the flawed but more powerful Christianity that I was coming to know through Flying Eagle.

About 10:00 A.M. Flying Eagle found me and sat down beside me. "You should not sit too long in the sun," he said. "It will make you funny in the head."

"I have been thinking about what you have been telling me about Christianity. It is really making sense now."

"Good," he said.

"But there is one thing that still troubles me. How is it that the Christian church could so easily abandon the part of its mission that called it to learn from others?"

"It is because you Christians did not take the role of the warrior seriously. In the early years of Christianity there were wide boundaries. Paul writes about the Church having a mission to the whole world and there are also indications in his writings that the church was being greatly affected by the Greek and Roman cultures that it was encountering as Christianity spread. But as the church lost its warriors and the boundaries became more narrow, Christians came to believe that they had all of the truth instead of an important part of the truth. When the boundaries are too narrow people make themselves right by making others wrong.

"In the Old Testament period there were prophets. The prophets were the warriors. Warriors are not always popular but they are always needed. The Christian church, however, has frequently ignored its prophets or has tried to silence them by looking for something wrong with their words and declaring them to be heretics. Some of the heretics were wrong but they were also warriors who were fighting to keep the boundaries of Christianity wide. You can be wrong and still be a good warrior. The truth is not in the words but in the silence between the words. As the warriors were ignored or silenced, the boundaries became more narrow. The Church started acting more concerned about being right than about finding the truth. In doing that, it abandoned the listening portion of its mission."

"Flying Eagle, you seem to know an awful lot about Christianity, more than anyone would know from just having read the Bible. How did you learn so much about it?"

"After Star Man showed me his wounds I became very interested in Christianity. I read many books about it. I thought about getting baptized and I am embarrassed to say that I even thought about becoming a minister, until Star Man talked me out of it. I thought that I had to abandon the religion of my people in order to find the truth. Like you, I came looking to find the truth in another religion. But in the search I came to understand my own religion more fully and I found that the truth was also between the words of the religion of my people."

"Do you ever wish that you had become a Christian?"

"Not any more. I learned a great deal from Christianity but when I made the discovery that the truth is not in the words of any religion, I became content.

He sighed and pursed his lips. He seemed deep in thought about what he was going to say next. "Just one thing more," he said finally. "When I told you that you needed to become a warrior, you thought I meant that you were going to have to kill something. You, my friend, are called by the Spirit to be a warrior of a different sort. You are called to fight for broad boundaries in your own religion. Do that and the truth will set you free." He rose and headed back in the direction of the village. He called back, "Remember. Don't sit too long in the sun. It will make you even funnier in the head."

⚴ 35 ⚵

I took Flying Eagle's advice about moving out of the sun and headed slowly back down the trail toward the village. I felt both surprised and relieved by Flying Eagle's statement that my calling as a warrior was to defend wide boundaries in Christianity. I had expected that I was going to be asked to engage in some sort of life threatening combat, a thought that was not totally appealing to me even as the warrior, Screaming Hawk. But there was something appealing to me about being a warrior for broad boundaries in Christianity. The more I thought about it, the more the idea intrigued me.

When I saw Flying Eagle in the village later that day I told him that I liked the idea. He smiled and said, "Good. It is better when one likes his calling than when one does not. The river flows. One can follow it or not. One can like it or not. When one likes the direction of the river and decides to follow it, it can be a delightful journey. But we will talk about that journey later.

"Screaming Hawk, there is a question that you have been wanting to ask me for some time. Now I will answer it."

"I want to know about the eagle that I saw the day we talked on the mountain top. Was that you?"

"Yes," he said.

"Teach me to fly!" I blurted out, surprising myself by the urgency and excitement that I felt. The idea of making that request hadn't even occurred to me before that moment.

"O.K.," he said simply.

With that brief exchange a process began that proved to be the most fascinating part of my entire apprenticeship with Flying Eagle. We met daily for the next few weeks. Each session was devoted almost entirely to issues related to flying.

"I am teaching you how to fly," he had said in the first of our sessions, "because in learning to fly you will have to master all of the skills that are needed to transform yourself into whatever you truly want to be. Flying does not come naturally to man, but it is possible. The way of the Spirit does not come naturally to man either but it too is possible. No one can learn to fly without also learning to manage his own unwieldy spirit. The reason that you can not fly now is that you have not let yourself fully become Screaming Hawk. I will start by teaching you how to scream.

"Scream," he said.

"What?"

"Scream now."

"Now?"

"Yes, now. You are Screaming Hawk. So scream!"

I let out a little shriek. I felt extremely self-conscious.

"You sounded like a 80 year old woman who has a lover with cold hands. Try again."

"Again?"

"Yes, again. Is something wrong with your hearing?"

I tried again.

"That was worse than before. If you burst into my lodge and gave that scream I wouldn't even bother to look up from my breakfast. I want to hear a war cry! Try it again."

"Again?"

"Yes, damn it! Again!"

I really did try. I mustered all my energy and tried to put it into a convincing scream.

Flying Eagle looked disgusted. "Not much better. If you are going to be a warrior you are going to have to learn to scream like one. Did you know that the South won some of its battles in the Civil War because its soldiers knew how to scream. The Rebel Yell, when properly done, could create stark terror among enemy troops. But your scream wouldn't even get their attention. I want you to go into the forest and practice. Practice every day until you get it. It is important. Go now and practice."

"Now?" I said smiling.

Flying Eagle let out a big sigh of exasperation. "Yes, now."

I headed off toward the forest. I looked over my shoulder and saw Flying Eagle shaking his head to himself as he walked up the steps to his lodge.

❧ 36 ❧

I headed deep into the forest. I didn't want anybody to be able to hear me practicing my scream. I whooped and shrieked and screeched. Not having an audience helped but I still felt ridiculous. After an hour I was getting too hoarse to continue, so I returned to the village.

At our session the next day Flying Eagle asked for a progress report on the scream.

"I worked on it yesterday but I don't think I made much progress," I said.

"Part of the problem is that you do not yet know how to become your scream. Until you can become your own scream there is not much hope for you being able to become an animal that can fly."

"But how do I become my scream?"

"First of all by giving up the notion that you are who you are. You are not who you are. Only the Spirit is who it is. You are who you can become and you can become what you are open to becoming. You were Little Warrior. You became open to becoming Screaming Hawk, so you are becoming Screaming Hawk. You become your scream the same way. First, you must realize that who you are is not fixed. It can be changed. Next you must will to become something different, in this case your scream. Finally you must let go of who you think you are and let yourself become what you will to become. It is then that you will find yourself in your own scream. You become the scream. The scream is not then just an expression of you, it will be you. The same power that you now have the scream will have. Is that clear?"

"Not exactly. Are you saying that I will be transformed into the scream itself?"

"Yes."

"Then what will happen to me?"

"What do you mean?"

"What will happen to my body when I become the scream?"

"Screaming Hawk, your question tells me that you still think that you are your body. You think that you are that ugly collection of meat, bone and hair that we have been calling Screaming Hawk. You are that body only because you choose to be. But you can also choose to be your scream."

"O.K. But where will that beautiful collection of meat, bone and hair be while I am the scream?"

"I, as the observer, will see that ugly collection of meat, bone and hair standing there producing the scream but I will not experience you in that body. I will experience you as truly being the scream. You yourself will not experience yourself as being in that body either. You will experience yourself as being the scream.

"A really good musician," he continued, "can reach a point where he is so fully identifying with the music he is playing that he becomes the music. I have been present when that has happened. Perhaps you have too. The musician's body is still there producing the music but the musician is no longer in his body; he is in the music. When we use the drums in our ceremonies the same thing happens; many of the drummers become the beat and the dancers become the dance. Have you never experienced what I am talking about?"

"Come to think of it, maybe I have. Once when I was playing in a tennis match I became so absorbed in the game that I lost awareness of myself and for a short while it was like what you are describing. I didn't have to think about the game or try to control my body to hit the ball. My body continued to hit the ball and I even made shots that I normally would have missed, but it didn't feel like I was playing the game. For that period I think maybe I really was the game. It was a strange experience that I have never been able to explain to anyone before."

"That's what I'm talking about. And that's what needs to happen when you scream."

"O.K. but I'm not sure how I did it before or how to do it again."

"That's why we are talking. I'm going to teach you.

"Part of what you discovered," he continued," was that you do not have to be in your body. You can be other places or be other things. You can be the game, the music or even a flying bird. But to be those things you must first be able to be yourself. The doorway into being something else is to be yourself. For you to fly you must first become Screaming

Hawk, the warrior. When you have fully become who you already are, you have the power to become whatever else you might choose to be.

"The universe was set up by the Spirit in such a way that when we have achieved one level of experience other possibilities become immediately open to us. The creation is constantly changing and re-creating itself, and you, as part of the creation, can and should experience re-creation as well. Re-creation is part of the process of personal and spiritual growth."

"But if I become a flying bird don't I give up my human characteristics to do that? Why do you call that growth?"

"Growth does not occur through adding things. Growth in the Spirit occurs through giving up things. The whole point of becoming a bird is that you have to give up parts of yourself to allow that to happen. The parts of yourself that you give up are returned to the Spirit and re-created. They are then available to you from the Spirit in a new form when, and if, you need them. Freedom does not come through having more, and growth does not come from having more. Nothing can be added to a person who is already full. A person who carries around lots of parts of himself has less available to him from the Spirit. Freedom comes through having less. When you have less, more is available to you. Be that which is simple. Be it fully. Then everything is available to you."

"Now you are confusing me again."

"Don't listen with your mind. Listen with your heart. What I am telling you is that the holy man is not holy because he has collected a lot of ideas, knowledge or experience. He is holy because he knows how to empty himself. He can become simple. It is becoming simple that is difficult, but becoming simple gives life. Give up the parts of yourself that you most value and you will discover that they always belonged to the Spirit anyway and not to you. In giving them up they become available to you again, but available as the Spirit's possession rather than your own. Being simple but having everything available; that is freedom.

"I can see that you are still confused. You will understand these things in time. You do not have to understand them now. Now you need to know only that it is through giving up things, including parts of yourself, that you achieve true freedom to be yourself. When you are free to give up the parts of yourself that are not a bird in order to become a bird, you are also free to become Screaming Hawk, the warrior. That is why I am teaching you to fly."

❦ 37 ❧

We continued to meet daily. Every afternoon I returned to the forest to practice screaming. My scream was getting louder with practice but little else about it had changed.

Then one day it started to happen. Instead of trying to make myself be my scream, I tried allowing myself to be my scream. I yielded somewhat and noticed that the awareness of my body seemed to fade slightly during some of the screams. Then I put less focus on producing a loud scream and continued screaming. The feeling that I was fading out intensified. Finally I gave up all my efforts to produce a good scream and just let the scream be whatever it would be. I experienced a sudden surge of energy that had been lacking before, a feeling of freedom accompanied by a sense of total focus and involvement. I felt myself surging forth with each scream and returning to my body as the scream stopped. It was exhilarating. Nothing seemed of importance except the scream. Nothing seemed important and yet everything seemed important. All of my being seemed to be contained in the scream. I felt free, whole and connected to the universe. The feeling lingered as I returned to my body each time for another breath. I screamed and screamed. It was fun. I felt exhilarated and cleansed.

As I was screaming, an eagle flew down and landed on one of the limbs of a tree not far from where I was standing. I looked at the eagle but continued to scream. He sat quietly watching me for a while and then flew off in the direction of the village.

I screamed for perhaps another hour and then walked briskly back down the long trail to the village. I felt wonderful. As I emerged from the forest Flying Eagle was waiting for me.

"That was wonderful!" he said.

"You were there weren't you."

"Yes. I could sense that you were having a good day practicing in the forest and decided to join you. I couldn't hear you from here so I figured that you must be a long way away. In those situations I have found that flying comes in handy. I hope you didn't mind."

"Not at all. It was nice to have your company, but I was having such a wonderful time I didn't want to stop screaming to talk to you."

"I understand. The first time I broke through and really screamed, I screamed the whole day. My parents got worried and organized a search party for me when I didn't come home for dinner. They found me sitting on a hillside two miles from the village, laughing and screaming. They thought something was wrong with me even though I told them that I was fine. They took me to the medicine man and he explained to them what had happened."

Flying Eagle looked deep into my eyes. "How are you feeling?"

"Wonderful! Absolutely wonderful!"

"Being simple is powerful isn't it."

"Yes. I feel powerful, clean, whole and at peace all at the same time."

"That feeling will not last. The experience is not about feelings, but it is always nice when the feelings come with an experience like that. Now you are closer to being ready to fly. We will talk more tomorrow."

❧ 38 ❧

When we met together the next day Flying Eagle said, "It is not time for you to start your primary work as a warrior. That will come after you leave this village and return to your people. The way of the warrior is difficult. Many people do not understand what the warrior does or the importance of his work. At times it is a lonely path to travel and there are few companions along the way. Out of loneliness, many warriors are tempted to join others with similar views and work together. At times, that can be a helpful way to promote a cause but, in the final analysis, the warrior faces death alone and must defend the boundaries alone. If one is seeking the agreement of others one can not be an effective warrior. The warrior knows what is right within himself and follows that. You are relieved that your role as warrior is not calling you into physical combat. I assure you that the dangers in the work that you will be doing are just as great and the times of fear just as intense as the warrior going into combat with a knife, a club or a rifle. Do not forget that you are a warrior. Because you will not be seeing the weapons of war does not mean that the combat is not mortal. It is and the suffering can be great."

"You don't paint a pretty picture of what's ahead for me."

"No, it is not pretty but it is glorious and you will find strength that you didn't know you had and you will find power that comes not from yourself. The true warrior is aided by the Spirit in ways that are truly astounding. The warrior's life is difficult but it is exciting and it means living in relationship to the Spirit in a very special way. You are called to that life. It will be difficult but it will be glorious.

"You want to learn to fly. Now that you know how to scream we can move deeper into the process. The first thing that you must remember, as I told you before, is that you are not who you think you are. Everything is in a state of becoming except the Spirit. The Spirit is. You may remember that in the Bible, God refers to himself as 'I am.' The Spirit is in the eternal present. You however are in a state of becoming. You are related to the Spirit but what you experience as being yourself are only the parts that are not yet complete, that are still becoming. To put it another way, you think that you are 'I am' but you are not; you are 'I will be.' As you move toward completion you will no longer be aware of the completed parts of yourself because they will have become Spirit. The only parts of yourself that you can experience as being yourself are the parts that are incomplete. Growth is, therefore, the process of becoming increasingly aware of the parts of yourself that are incomplete and different from the Spirit. The hypocrite pretends that he is already complete and tries to live out of that pretended completeness. In so doing the hypocrite both severs his relationship with the Spirit and denies who he, himself, really is. One must be aware of his incompleteness and live out of that to truly be oneself. The parts that are complete are encountered through the Spirit. The parts that are incomplete are encountered by being oneself. The mission of all of us is to become reunited with the Spirit, to lose ourselves within the Spirit and thereby be complete. There are religions of the East that speak more directly about this process than does Christianity. There were Christian theologians who tried to address this process of being reunited with the Spirit, but they were often treated with contempt or declared to be heretics. Their works were destroyed or largely ignored. Christianity is currently incomplete in this area. To be complete it must absorb some of the knowledge of the truth found in the Eastern religions. So far there has been a great deal of resistance to doing that. That Christianity has not yet absorbed those truths does not mean that a Christian can not follow the path of gradually reuniting with the Spirit, but the Christian who does not have knowledge of other faiths may have difficulty understanding the process that is happening to him.

"The power to fly does not come out of the is; it comes out of the becoming. I realize that what I am explaining to you may seem confusing but it is important and you must understand it in order to fly. Focus on becoming. You will only be a bird as long as you are becoming a bird. In other words, you can only become a bird by engaging in the process of becoming that part of the Spirit that the bird represents. You, Screaming Hawk, have a hawk as a power animal. The power animal's function is to help you with the process of developing into that which you are becoming. While you are truly in the process of becoming what the hawk represents, you will have the capability of becoming a hawk and of flying as a hawk. Once you have fully achieved being all that the hawk represents you will no longer find yourself able to be a hawk and will find

⚘ 39 ⚘

We continued to meet daily. Flying Eagle's instructions repeatedly stressed the importance of giving up parts of myself, of becoming simple, and of living out of becoming. The teaching sessions were becoming tedious for me. I started to dread our meetings and yet continued to meet with Flying Eagle at the appointed time each day. Finally I had had enough and complained openly about it.

"Flying Eagle, you have been telling me the same things over and over in different ways for the past two weeks. I'm getting tired of this. I don't want to be here. It's a waste of time and I'm getting really irritated about it."

"Oh," he said. "Why are you here?"

"To learn how to fly."

"Have your learned to fly yet?"

"No."

"Then we must continue." And he started into another one of his long rambling explanations about giving up parts of oneself, about becoming simple and about living out of becoming. I interrupted him.

"Damn it! There you go again. You are telling me all the same things over and over again. I have heard this a hundred times now."

"What do you want?"

"I want you to get on with it. I want you to teach me how to fly."

"Have you flown yet?"

"No."

"Then we must continue." He started going over the same points he had gone over before. I interrupted again.

"But you haven't told me anything new in two weeks."

"That is correct." And he continued with the same material.

"Stop! I can't take this any more! Tell me how to fly!"

"That's what I have been telling you for the past two weeks. I have been telling you how to fly. You keep sitting here like there is more that you need to know. So we go over it again. When are you going to get it through your thick skull that there is no more. You already know all you need to know. You want to fly? So fly!" He stood up abruptly and headed back to the village alone.

I sat and thought for a long time. I thought about giving up parts of myself, about becoming simple and about living out of becoming. Then I remembered my power animal. I had not talked to the hawk for quite a while. Since his function was to help me become, I decided to call upon him. I sat quietly and waited.

Perhaps thirty minutes later I heard the soft sound of flapping wings and glanced up just in time to see the hawk land a few feet away from me. I waited in silence. A few minutes later he spoke.

"You have called me and I have come," he said. "What do you want?"

"I want to fly."

"So fly," he said simply as though there was nothing more that needed to be said.

"But I need help. Flying Eagle taught me that I must get rid of parts of myself, that I must become simple and that I must live out of becoming. I understand all that but I need someone to lead me through the process. I called on you for that purpose."

"You do not need me for that. You can fly without my assistance."

"Maybe so. But I feel excited and scared and lonely. It really would be helpful to have you lead me through this."

"Well, since I'm already here I might as well help," he said with surprising patience.

"Thank you," I said, feeling very much relieved.

"I felt those same things the first time I tried to fly. My mother had been telling me for days how to do it. 'Flap your wings and will yourself to move forward through the air,' she had said. 'The rest will take care of itself.' I knew how to do that but I was scared. I wanted her to be there with me, to tell me again what I already knew. She was patient. She stayed with me most of that morning. I flapped and flapped. Finally I willed myself into the air while I was flapping and flew, actually flew from the nest to the ground! I was elated. That was the most exciting day of my life. I was finally a bird who could fly!

"My mother was patient with me. She taught me over and over what I needed to do. I could have flown without her being there, but I wanted her there and she stayed. I will stay with you.

"There are many different ways to follow the process Flying Eagle taught you. The method you choose is of little importance as long as the process itself is followed. I will lead you through just one of the many ways.

"You must first empty yourself. You must let go of all those things that you think are you. If you want to save your life you must lose it. You are still holding onto your life, holding on to who you think you are, holding on to what is of value to you. Let go of all that. Let yourself slip into nothingness. There you will find your true self, in nothingness. It does not take long. It is simply a matter of letting go. When you let go you can slide into nothingness quickly."

I did as he suggested. I allowed myself to slip into nothingness. It was easier than I had expected. For a moment, as all those parts that I had thought were me slipped away, I felt panic and a strong urge to stop the process. But I resisted the urge and was absorbed into a great ocean of calm. I was relaxed. It was peaceful. There was nothingness.

I cannot explain it, but in the nothingness I was still me. I was no longer any of the things that I had thought were me but I still existed. It was strange and mysterious and wonderful.

Then the hawk spoke again.

"You have given up all the parts of yourself. Now you must choose out of the nothingness only a few parts of Screaming Hawk that you wish to become more fully at this moment. Since you want to fly, you must choose only things that Screaming Hawk, the man, shares with the animal nature of all hawks. If you choose any characteristics that hawks do not possess, it will prevent you from flying."

He was quiet again. I chose the qualities of daring, determination and cunning. After more silence he continued.

"You are now simple. You are free of the parts that are not the hawk. You are ready to become. Let yourself go deeper. Let yourself be reborn as a hawk who is in the process of becoming the qualities that you seek. Do not resist the urge to become. Yield to it. Allow yourself to emerge as a new creature and experience life in a new way."

I felt a change taking place in my being. There was a tremendous urge to emerge, to express myself, to burst forth into a new realm. And it happened. It was like walking out of a cave into bright sunlight and seeing for the first time the world as it exists above ground. Everything was new. Everything was fresh. Everything was beautiful.

I found myself standing beside the hawk, but I was the same size as a hawk. I had become a hawk.

"Join me now as we fly together," he said.

I felt power in my wings. I moved them and felt my feet being lifted off the ground as I flapped my wings in sheer ecstasy. We moved up into the air, through the trees and up into the cloudless sky. I could see for miles. I felt free, whole and complete. We twisted and turned together as I experienced the freedom of being able to head any direction I chose or to circle on the rising cushion of air that was being blown up the face of the mountain. We flew for perhaps an hour, climbing, circling, diving and then skimming along at treetop level looking for game. Without uttering a word we finally turned toward the small clearing in the woods where we had met and glided in for a landing.

"You have done well," he said. "You will become a man again. But you will be different." With that parting comment he turned his head and flew off through the trees leaving me alone in the forest.

I suddenly felt exhausted. I closed my eyes and immediately fell asleep.

❧ 40 ❧

I woke up lying on my face in the leaves of the forest floor. I had no idea how long I had been asleep. It could have been years or only a moment.

I rose and walked back to the village. When I arrived I saw Flying Eagle sitting in a chair in front of his lodge.

"How did it go?" he called as I approached him.

I told him in detail about my experience. He smiled and nodded at various points as I filled him in on my adventure.

"It was the most amazing experience of my life," I said, concluding my narration. "But there is one thing that puzzles me."

"What's that?"

"I woke up lying on the ground in the forest. Could all of this have been a dream? It seemed so real."

"It was real," he said simply. "This afternoon I saw two hawks circling above the mountain. I knew that one of them was you. The reason that you fell asleep was because you are new to the experience of becoming an animal. As you gain experience in this area you will no longer fall asleep to make the transition back to being a man. Do not doubt your experience. It was real.

"There is something that you should know," he continued. "You chose daring, determination and cunning when you became a hawk this time. You will find that those qualities have strengthened within you as a result of becoming a hawk. But don't rely too heavily on this method of personal growth. It is only one way to grow. Use it, but use it sparingly. It is better to grow in many different ways than just one way.

"I also want to caution you to be careful about who you tell about your experience. Some will not understand. Some White Men assume that all Indians understand the things of the Spirit because they are Indians. That is not true. When I flew as an eagle for the first time I was young. I was so excited that I told some of my friends about it. They, of course, were

Indians, but they did not understand. Some thought I was crazy. Others thought I was lying. Sometimes they would laugh when I came around. They called me Bird Face. I learned to choose carefully who I told about my experiences. I suggest that you do the same."

"How did you learn to fly?" I asked.

"That is a long story. I will tell you a shortened version of it. I was a young man. It was not long after I met Star Man for the first time. He had told me about flying but I had not understood. I thought he meant that I could fly in my mind. I didn't realize that I could actually fly physically. I spent many weeks focusing on the things that I told you to do. I will not review them again. You have finally learned them. Anyway, as I was saying, I thought that I was going to fly in my mind. One day I was meditating by myself on the side of a hill. After the experience of nothingness I felt my body become small. I did not know what was happening. My arms felt funny and when I turned my head to look at them I discovered that I had wings, that I had become an eagle. It scared me. I was an eagle for perhaps five minutes before I fell asleep and woke up as a person again. I didn't try to fly that day; I was too confused by what happened to me. When I woke up I ran to the medicine man's lodge and told him what had happened. He was very pleased and explained to me that those who follow the path of the Spirit can become animals when they choose. I did not believe him at first, but he convinced me that it is true. Later it happened to me again. That time I did fly and it was wonderful."

"Did you study under the medicine man?"

"Yes. After I flew for the first time I went to him and told him that I wanted to become a medicine man. I became his student and his friend. He taught me many things about the ways of my people and about the Spirit.

"We met together for many years. Even after I had become a medicine man myself we would get together from time to time to discuss what we had learned about the Spirit. I loved him. He was closer to me than my own father. When he died, I cried. I still miss him sometimes even though he has been with our ancestors for many years.

"Once shortly after he died he appeared to me. He told me that we were right; that life does go on after death. He said that the land of our ancestors is glorious and to be there is more wonderful than to fly as an eagle. It was good to see him again. It made the pain of losing him easier. I have not seen him again. But he told me that he would be waiting for me and I long for that time when we will meet and talk again about the ways of the Spirit." Flying Eagle was crying now. Large tears rolled down his face and fell onto his shirt.

"I will say good-bye to you soon. You must return to your people and teach them the ways of the Spirit. Some of them will listen to you. Those who hear will learn that the realm of the Spirit is as real as the physical realm and they will learn from you how to experience the power of both in the present moment. That is what you are called to teach, to defend wide boundaries and to teach about both realms.

"I have taught you much about the Spirit, but there is more to know. Some things I will teach you at a later time. Some you must learn on your own. And do not forget Star Man; he may choose to teach you some things himself.

"Be open to the truth wherever you find it. The Spirit speaks in many ways, to many peoples, in many languages. I have taught you much of what I know. It is time now for you to go and learn from those you teach. Listen to them. You will hear the Spirit in their questions and you will find the Spirit in their experiences and beliefs. You are called to teach, but most of all you are called to learn from those you teach.

"In a few days we will say good-bye for now. Do not forget what you have learned. Do not forget to share it. And do not forget to love those whom you teach. Star Man would have it no other way."

He walked into his lodge and closed the door.

❧ 41 ❧

The thought of leaving Flying Eagle brought a deep sense of sadness. I did not feel ready, but I knew that he was right, that it was time for me to leave and start my work as a warrior and a teacher. Our remaining time together passed quickly. The sessions now focused mostly on preparing for the work that lay ahead of me.

"You will be moving into a new phase of your life," he said in our last session together. "The life of the warrior is different. You do not yet feel fully ready for that life. That is good, for you are still in the process of becoming a warrior. If you were already fully a warrior there would be no power in your life. You must live out of becoming. Do not forget that. If you wait until you are fully ready for anything then you will cease to be ready. You are ready when you are not quite ready. You are ready when you know enough to start your work but do not know enough to finish it without becoming.

"We will talk again. I will teach you more later, but for now you must leave here and start your own work. Tomorrow we will say good-bye. I will miss you, Screaming Hawk. You have become important to me. When you leave you will take a part of me with you.

"I do not want you to contact me for six months. A warrior must learn to work alone. I will think of you often but we will not talk. Later we can talk and you can tell me what you have learned.

"If you need assistance call on your power animal. He is available to you. But remember that it is important to grow in many different ways and to learn from the Spirit not through one source alone but through many. Your students will teach you; your friends will teach you; life itself will teach you. The truth comes in many different ways. It always comes when one is open and truly seeking it. And when it comes it comes without words. It comes not to be spoken but to be experienced. It is found in the silence between the words."

❧ 42 ☙

I arose early on my last day in the village. I packed my suitcase and loaded it into the car as the sun was beginning to peep over the top of the distant mountains. Flying Eagle met me at the car.

"Do you have time for a walk before you go?" he asked.

"Yes," I replied.

We headed into the forest as we had so many times before. This time there was no teaching, no words, just a long walk in silence between two friends, enjoying each other's presence and sharing the power of the moment. The forest was alive with activity as the animals were beginning this new day. As we walked, I thought about the past months that I had spent with Flying Eagle and how strange it was that I had come to him originally to learn only about his religion. I had learned far more than I had ever bargained for. I was deeply grateful and he knew it.

When we returned to the car he spoke.

"Many years ago I was given something that I have shown to no one. I want you to have it as you start your new life as a warrior. Take it with you and remember."

He pulled something out of his pocket and thrust it into my hand. It was a single, perfectly formed eagle feather made of silver.

"Star Man gave this to me," he said. "I want you to have it now. Don't forget him.

"Go in peace, my brother," he said and gave me a hug.

"Thank you for everything," I said as I hugged him back."

I drove away from the village feeling intense grief over leaving Flying Eagle, my teacher and my friend. He had touched my life in many ways and I had been changed.

I was ready now to start my work as a warrior, ready to start but not yet ready to meet all its challenges. I was becoming.

About the Author

Patton Boyle is an Episcopal priest and pastoral counselor/psychothera-pist. He currently lives in Oregon with his wife and two daughters, where he has a counseling practice, conducts workshops, and writes books about the path of spiritual growth and discovery.

The author may be contacted through Station Hill Press, Station Hill Rd., Barrytown, New York, 12507.

Also Available from Station Hill

Shaking Out the Spirits
A Psychotherapist's Entry
into the Healing Mysteries of Global Shamanism
Bradford Keeney

Bradford Keeney's extraordinary odyssey began in 1971, when, as a respected professor, pyschotherapist, and author, he found himself suddenly visited, without the influence of hallucinogenic drugs or shamanic teachings, by remarkable visions of "shamanic realities" that called him to some of the most remote areas of the world. Shepherded on his journey by the spirit of the Oglala Sioux medicine man Black Elk (whose time of death was virtually the same as Keeney's birth), Keeney was initiated into the healing practices of tribal peoples in North and South America, of Christians in the African-American sanctified church, of sangomas, sanusis, and healers throughout Africa (among them the Bushmen of the Kalahari and the Zulu of Southern Africa), and finally of the only living masters of a pre-Buddhist healing art in Japan. Illuminated with the author's own photographs of his life among the shamans, and blessed by elder healers throughout the world (who passed along not only their sacred knowledge but their spirit guides as well), Keeney's story gives voice to the mind, heart, and soul of shamanic healing.
Bradford Keeney is the author of 11 books, inlcuding *Aesthetics of Change, Mind in Therapy: Constructing Systemic Family Therapies*, and *Constructing Theapeutic Realities: Praxis and Theory*.
   $13.95 paper, ISBN 0-88268-164-8, 6 x 9, 216 pages, 40 b&w photos.

Sam Woods
American Healing
Stan Rushworth

This unusual and eloquent book is not about healing technique, but is an extraordinary exploration into the healing spirit. Weaving together prayers and stories, *Sam Woods* reveals a fascinating world of healings, revelation and discovery through healing, and attitudes toward healing; the book becomes a healing unto itself as we begin to feel and see the way Sam Woods moves through his life. With prayer and praise, illumination and judgment, a healer's view of living today is opened to us, and we see how we are drawn to fall away from the Earth, and how we come back. Sam Woods says, "This book is a joining, a listening to the voices of the earth, of the hawk and frog, of the children, of the people. It is a long prayer, a gathering together, a quiet walk into seeing, carrying everything with us as we go, our history, our ancestors, our sorrow, and our promise."
   $11.95 paper, ISBN 0-88268-122-2, 5½ x 8½, 192 pages.

Death Is of Vital Importance
On Life, Death, and Life After Death
ELISABETH KUBLER-ROSS, M.D.

These intimate, conversational talks, edited from speaking engagements, offer an over-view of the life and work of a woman who has been as influential as she is remarkable. Enlivened with dozens of striking case histories and memorable stories from the author's own childhood, the book recounts such events as her extraordinary meeting with a woman in the German concentration camp of Maidanek a few months after the war, her mother's death, and her own near-death experience and epiphany of "cosmic conscious-ness." Also included is a step-by-step breakdown of the experience of dying, descriptions of the differences among physical, psychic, and spiritual energy and of her method for interpreting children's drawings, based on Jung's theory (and later expanded by Dr. Bernie Siegel). She offers insights into the now-famous *Dougy* letter, and proposes the establishment of ET (elderly-toddler) centers, where children can be "spoiled rotten." At the end of this special book, readers will feel that they have spent a privileged evening in the presence of a wonderful and very wise woman.

Elisabeth Kubler-Ross, author of the international bestseller *On Death and Dying*, has been one of the most prominent pioneers of the hospice movement. Her farm near Staunton, Virginia, is also a retreat and workshop center.

$12.95 paper. ISBN 0-88268-186-9; 216 pages, 6 x 9, bibliography.

Thunder's Grace
Walking the Road of Visions with My Lakota Grandmother
MARY ELIZABETH THUNDER

Abandoned by her mother when she was three weeks old, Mary Elizabeth Thunder survived abuse, a broken marriage, and a heart attack to become one of the most highly esteemed leaders in the Native American movement — healer, visionary, teacher, and chosen successor in a native tradition. Her story is also the true tale of a remarkable elder, Grandma Grace Spotted Eagle, who adopted her and guided her to spiritual awakening as a messenger. At once harrowing and uplifting, this memoir takes us from her early life and experiences with the legendary elders Chief Leonard Crow Dog, Wallace Black Elk, and Rolling Thunder, through the near-death experiences that utterly transformed her, to nine remarkable years spent traveling America by van, culminating in her inclusion in the Sun Dance, one of the world's oldest and most venerable initiation ceremonies. Intimate, painfully honest, essentially and overwhelmingly spiritual, this is a book about a woman's quest for meaning amid two cultures and a compelling account of the visionary underpin-nings of Native American life.

Mary Elizabeth Thunder, well known for her part in opening traditional spirituality to non-Native peoples, conducts vision quests and sweat lodges around the country and runs the Thunder Horse Ranch in West Point, Texas,

$14.95 paper. ISBN 0-88268-166-4; 256 pages, 40 b/w photos, index, bibliography.